The Eridanos Library 9

Pierre Klossowski

The Baphomet

Translated by Sophie Hawkes and
Stephen Sartarelli.

Eridanos Press

Contents

Introduction

by Juan García Ponce

Pierre Klossowski, whose life and works are without question exceptional and extreme, was born in Paris on August 9, 1905. His father, a German of Polish descent, was an art critic and enjoyed the friendship of Bonnard, to whom he had devoted a long study. His mother, Baladine Klossowska, was a painter. The outbreak of World War I forced the family to move to Geneva where Klossowski received a strict Catholic and classical education. The poet, and friend of the family, Rainer Maria Rilke, presented the first exhibition of drawings by Pierre Klossowski's older brother, the painter Balthus who was then ten years old, an exhibition devoted to studies of his cat, Mitsou. Recommended to André Gide by Rilke, Pierre Klossowski moved to Paris a few years after the war. Gide helped him begin drama studies in Vieux Colombier, employed him as his secretary, and introduced him to the literary world where he met, among others, Paulhan, Groethuyscn, Cassou, and Jouve with whom he was to publish in 1929 a translation of Hölderlin's *Poems of Madness*. Gide used to urge Klossowski to keep him meticulously informed of his homosexual adventures, to the point that Klossowski says he ended up inventing some to satisfy his benefactor.

Later, he became associated with Doctor Laforgue and Maria Bonaparte in the founding of the first Psychoanalytical Society, met André Breton, and participated with Georges Bataille, whose friendship he had enjoyed since 1934, in the sessions of the College de Sociologie directed by Bataille himself, Michel Leiris, and Roger Callois. At the suggestion of Jean Wahl, he published essays on Sade in the review *Recherches Philosophiques*. A violent religious crisis caused him to withdraw from the world and become a Dominican novice, enrolling in the Catholic schools of Lyon and Paris. After spending all the war years as a religious novice, he returned to lay life in 1945. In 1947, he married Denise Morin-Sinclaire and published *Sade man Prochaine*. His first work of fiction, *La Vocation Suspendue*, written as if it were a novel's critical study, appeared two years later and is, to a great extent, an autobiographical confession about the failure of his religious vocation. In 1954, Klossowski published his second novel, *Roberte ce Soir*, illustrated with five of his drawings. In it, for the first time, the figure of Roberte emerges as "the only sign," true sexual symbol and the so-called Lois de l'Hospitalité—the giving of one's wife to the guests of the house—become established. This work was described by Georges Bataille as "beyond the limits." *La Révocation de l'Edict de Nantes* appeared in 1959, followed the next year by *Le Souffleur ou le Théâtre de la Société*. The three books, all of which have Roberte as the protagonist, were published as a trilogy in 1965 under the title of *Les Lois de l'Hospitalité*. Roberte has by now been established as a sexual symbol and the centerpiece of Pierre Klossowski's work.

In 1956, Klossowski published a book impossible to classify, a mixture of mythic re-creation, religious essay, narrative work, creation of visual simulacra by means of verbal description: *Le Bain de Diane*. Diane in terms of physical appearance could be Roberte while Actaeon the hunter, obsessed with seeing and possessing the goddess of hunting, could, in terms of thought, represent Klossowski himself. But Diane, although visible and possessible through words, is nothing but the simulacrum of a goddess, a mere statuary figure, a "mongrel bitch," as Actaeon himself says at the moment of possessing her and destroying her with strikes from her hunting bow while she ascends to the heavens, turned into the lunar horn that adorns her hair: Actaeon, hunter, transformed to stag by the goddess and devoured by her dogs; Diana, possessible, not possessible. The only truth is the myth, the simulacrum created by words. In this case, as for the Greeks, sculpture or painting represented the gods venerated by the mortals.

Klossowski's essays on various authors and works were published in a volume titled, after a verse of Virgil, *Un si Funeste Désire*. A small exclusivist press, Fata Morgana, published *Origines Cultuelles et Mythiques d'un certain Comportement des Dames Romaines*, Klossowski's study of sacred prostitution in ancient Rome, as well as his essay *Sade and Fourier*, accompanied by a divertimento in homage of Gille Deleuze, *Les Derniers Travaux de Gulliver*, in which Roberte is once again the principal character. In 1965, Pierre Klossowski published his last novel, *Le Baphomet*, which won the discriminating Prix des Critiques. *Nietzsche et le Cercle Vicieux*, an extended philosophical book, at once biographical and psychological, composed of fragments, letters, and commentaries, appeared in 1969. Subsequently, Klossowski published an exceptional volume, *La Monnaie Vivante*, a parody of the economic essay taking as key figures Sade and Fourier and refuting the demoralizing power of the industrial society accompanied by drawings by the author and Pierre Zucca's photographs of "tableaux vivants" created by Klossowski and in which Denise Morin-Sinclaire is always the central figure.

Since then, Pierre Klossowski has dedicated himself primarily to painting and drawing. He uses for his large-format pictures colored pencils on paper covering almost obsessively large areas with a myriad of fine lines. The themes are often lascivious. Roberte appears in many of these works along with the character who will be transformed into a new god in *The Baphomet*. His paintings have been displayed in many major galleries throughout the world and won him the grand prize in one of the Documenta festivals in Kassen.

Pierre Zucca directed the film *Roberte*, an adaptation of *Roberte ce Soir* and *La Révocation de l'Edict de Nantes*. Pierre Klossowski played the part of Octave, the perverse husband in the novels, and his wife, Denise Morin-Sinclaire, that of Roberte. The filmscript, along with various drawings, photographs, and essays, has been published by the magazine *Obliques*.

In 1985, Jean-Maurice Monnoyer published *Le Peintre et son Démon*, a series of conversations with Pierre Klossowski in which the artist, although describing some of his drawings, hardly talks of painting but rather of his novels, his friends, his protectors, and his life.

Pierre Klossowski is a distinguished translator from Latin and German. His translations from Latin include: Suetonius's *Lives of the Caesars*, Virgil's *Aeneid*, the Inquisition papers of Gilles de Rais's trial, and works of Saint Augustine. Of his translations from German we must mention *The Gay Science* and *Posthum-*

ous Fragments (Autumn 1887-March 1888) for the definitive edition of Nietzsche's complete works compiled by Colli and Montinari, *The Biblical Meditations of Hamann*, Heidegger's *Nietzsche*, Wittgenstein's *Tractatus Logico-Philosophicus*, and the *Diaries* of Paul Klee.

Michel Foucault has written about Pierre Klossowski:

> . . . A perilous space is being opened where the discourse, the fables, the entangling and tangled traps of Klossowski are going to find a language of their own. A language for us as essential as those of Blanchot and Bataille. . . .

The Baphomet has been published in many languages and is now finally available in English in the translation by Sophie Hawkes who has faithfully rendered all the subtleties of Klossowski's intricate world. In the novel, the prologue is historical and takes place in 1307, just a few days before the destruction of the Templar Order brought about by the intrigues of Philip the Fair, King of France, but the fanciful treatment of this event is Klossowski's own. The rest of *The Baphomet* is a fantastic story set among the souls or "pure breaths" exhaled from the bodies that had contained them in life, in one of the fortress-convents of the Templar Order where the Thrones and Dominions, two categories of angels, have appointed Sir Jacques de Molay—last Grand Master of the Order condemned by the Inquisition and burned to death like so many of his brethren—guardian of the exhaled souls until the Last Judgment and the Resurrection of the flesh, events that will permit them to rejoin the bodies they occupied in life.

The novel consequently takes place almost entirely outside of time, so rather than fantastic, it would be more accurate to term it theological and metaphysical. In the prologue, Valentine de Saint-Vit, Lady of

Palençay—whose lands have been donated to the Templar Order, upon learning about the intrigue of the King, is trying to reclaim them by introducing her nephew, Ogier de Beauséant, into the order as a page, hoping that accusations could be brought based on the homosexuality of many of the monk-soldiers—and other main characters are surrounded by Templars who have the same names as those in Walter Scott's *Ivanhoe*. A parody of the historical novel. The questions that follow concern what may happen to the souls, the pure breaths, once they have lost the body that gave them an identity on earth. If these souls have no corporeal reality, if they are pure breaths, wouldn't they tend to mix, to lose themselves, producing a confusion of identities further compounded by a desire to reincarnate and attempt to insufflate themselves in bodies to be born, thus creating a problem of metempsychosis, which would be nothing more than another heresy? Realistically, the task given to Jacques de Molay by the Thrones and Dominions is not an easy one, especially bearing in mind that everything takes place outside of time and, therefore, the number of exhaled souls is in fact uncountable.

Nevertheless, Pierre Klossowski's narrative solution turns this metaphysical problem precisely into a novel in the strictest sense of the term. In *The Baphomet*, as Klossowski himself says in his "Notes and explanations," included in this edition of the novel, everything is a spectacle; language allows the creation of a series of images that can be admired by listening to that language.

The metaphysical speculation is not a pretext, but is converted through the intervention of the artist's work into something that has "body," a body of words, of pure breaths, just as the pure breaths, the souls, have body in the novel without losing their category of exhaled breaths. Thus the metaphysical verification occurs during one of the celebrations that the Templars observe each year on the anniversary of their execution also under the form of the description of a banquet in which we witness an array of wonders. As it progresses, the narrative method chosen by Pierre Klossowski allows for interruptions during one of which the greatest wonder takes place: the insufflation of the soul of Saint Theresa in the only body that appears in the metaphysical section of the novel: the dead but uncorrupted body of Ogier de Beauséant, resplendent with beauty, hands bound behind its back, hanging from a rope tied around its neck, at the time when Jacques de Molay is visiting the place where Ogier was executed in the historical section of the novel.

Anything can happen if language is capable of making it visible and, indeed, anything will happen until a new gnosis is created, a new form of knowledge that is in fact spectacle and as such offers itself to us. To achieve this , parallel to the speculation, several characters appear which are also historical and whose epochs can only coincide on the stage which is the novel: besides Sir Jacques de Molay and various members of the exterminated Templar Order, figures such as Frederic II of Hohenstaufen, Saint Theresa of Avila, Friedrich Nietzsche. To the fusion of separate epochs is added the fusion of names corresponding to separate persons, obviously misidentified by Jacques de Molay, who, just as it happened historically, receives during the banquet a visit from a Philip the Fair, accomplishing in fact an act of prestidigitation.

There is also, of course, the attraction of the Grand Master for the figure of Ogier de Beauséant as he approaches the banquet table seductively dressed in a

Templar page's robe. Not to mention the problem of metempsychosis raised by Saint Theresa by beseeching God to permit the reincarnation of her former confessor obsessed with carnal passion for her and reappearing in such guises as that of Bernini—who immediately creates a "despicable simulacrum" of the Saint in full amorous rapture, her heart pierced by an angel's arrow—and of a present-day soul (Klossowski's own?) who would have been pious but, excessively scrupulous, is granted for his fulfillment, to accompany him in his earthly days, a woman, an unbelieving one at that, whom he offers to his friends, the same way that Bernini offered the figure of Saint Theresa for all who viewed her statue to contemplate. Thus, the successive reincarnations only cause the original obsession to grow progressively greater.

Are there any solutions? The one that leaves no room for doubt—since for greater dramatic impact the spirit of Saint Theresa, carried upon a breeze, has revealed to the Grand Master, on the Isle des Vaches, as it is today in the center of Paris, that a cycle of history has come to an end and there will be no Final Judgment or Resurrection of the flesh, and thus the reason she wants to return to the old Templar fortress-convent, again turned into a soul, a pure breath, in the hope of meeting her former confessor once more—is knowledge achieved by reading the spectacle created by words, pure breaths, the pure breaths of the novelist, essayist, scholar Pierre Klossowski, whose means of knowledge emerge by reading him as what in the final analysis he truly is: a supreme artificer, a great artist.

Translated by Thomas Christensen and Juan García de Oteyza

The Prose of Actaeon

by Michel Foucault

Klossowski revives a long lost experience. Of this experience, hardly any vestiges remain that might call our attention to it; and those that do survive would no doubt remain enigmatic if they had not been given new vividness and prominence in Klossowski's language. And if, since then, they had not resumed speaking—saying that the Demon is not the Other, the opposite pole of God, the Antithesis without recourse (or almost), evil matter, but rather something strange and unsettling that leaves one baffled and motionless: the Same, the perfect Likeness.

Dualism and Gnosticism, despite all the denials and persecutions, have indeed borne heavily on the Christian conception of Evil: their binary mode of thought (God and Satan, Light and Darkness, Good and Heaviness, the great battle, and a certain radical, obstinate spitefulness) has organized, for our thought, the order of disorders. Western Christianity condemned Gnosticism, but from it retained a light, appealing form of reconciliation; for a long time, in its fantasies, it carried on the simplified duels of the Temptation: through the cracks in the world, a whole people of strange animals rises up before the half-open eyes of the kneeling anchorite—ageless figures of matter.

But what if, on the contrary, the Other were the Same? And the Temptation were not one episode of the great antagonism, but the meager insinuation of the Double? What if the duel took place inside a mirror's space? What if eternal History (of which our own is but the visible form, soon to be effaced) were not simply always the same, but the identity of this Same—at once the imperceptible displacement and the grip of the nondissociable? There is a vast range of Christian experience well familiar with this danger: the temptation to experience the temptation in the mode of the indiscernable. The quarrels of demonology are devoted to this profound danger; and consumed, or rather animated and multiplied by it, they are forever resuming an endless discussion: to go to the Sabbath is to surrender to the Devil, or perhaps also to devote oneself to the Devil's simulacrum which God has sent to tempt men of little faith—or men of too much faith, the credulous who imagine that there is another god than God. And the judges who burn the possessed are themselves victims of this temptation, this trap in which their justice becomes entangled: for those possessed are but a vain image of the false power of demons, an image by means of which the Demon takes possession not of the bodies of the sorcerers but of the souls of their executioners. Unless of course God himself has donned the face of Satan in order to becloud the spirits of those who do not believe in the uniqueness of his omnipotence; in which case God, in simulating the Devil, would bring about the odd espousal of the two condemned figures, the witch and her persecutor—both thereby consigned to Hell, to the reality of the Devil, to the true simulacrum of God's simulation of the Devil. In all these twists and turns the perilous games of extreme similitude multiply: God so closely resembling Satan who imitates God so well. . . .

It took no less than Descartes's Evil Genius to put an end to this great peril of Identities, over which 17th century thought had "subtilized" to no end. The Evil Genius of the Third Meditation is not a lightly seasoned compendium of the powers of deception residing within man, but he who most resembles God, who can imitate every one of His powers, can pronounce eternal verities like Him, and can, if he wishes, make two plus two equal five. He is His marvellous twin, except for a malignance that expels him immediately from all possible existence. Ever since then, the concern over simulacra has fallen into silence. We have even forgotten that until the beginning of the Neoclassical age (observe the literature and especially the theatre of the Baroque era) such simulacra constituted one of the great causes of vertigo for Western thought. We continued to worry about evil, about the reality of images and representation, and about the synthesis of the different. We no longer thought that the Same could still get the better of one's reason.

Incipit Klossowski, like Zarathustra. In this somewhat obscure and secret side of the Christian experience, he suddenly discovers (as if it were the latter's double, perhaps its simulacrum) the resplendent theophany of the Greek gods. Between the ignoble Goat who presents himself at the Sabbath and the virgin goddess who steals away into the water's coolness, the game is reversed: during Diana's bath, the simulacrum occurs in the flight from extreme proximity and not in the insistent intrusion of the other world. But the doubt is the same, as well as the risk of splitting in two: "Diana makes a pact with an intermediary demon between the gods and humanity to appear to Actaeon. By means of his airy form, the Demon *simulates* Diana in her theophany and inspires in Actaeon the desire and mad hope of possessing the goddess. He becomes the imagination and mirror of Diana." And Actaeon's final metamorphosis transforms him not into a hounded stag but into an impure, frantic and delightfully desecrating goat. As if, in the complicity of the divine in sacrilege, something of the light of Greece streaked with lightning the dark background of the Christian night.

Klossowski finds himself situated at the intersection of two very divergent and yet very similar paths, both originating in the Same, and both perhaps leading there as well: that of the theologians and that of the Greek gods, whose glorious return Nietzsche proclaimed to be imminent. The return of the gods, which is also, without any possible dissociation, the insinuation of the Demon into the unsavory, tepid night: "What, if some day or night a *demon* were to steal after you into your loneliest loneliness and say to you: 'This life as you now live it and have lived it, you will have to live once more and innumerable times more; and there will be nothing new in it, but every pain and joy and every thought and sigh and everything unutterably small or great in your life will return to you, all in the same succession and sequence—even this spider and this moonlight between the trees, and even this moment and *I myself.* The eternal hourglass of existence is turned upside down again and again, and you with it, speck of dust!' Would you not throw yourself down and gnash your teeth and curse the demon who spoke thus? Or have you once experienced a tremendous moment when you could reply to him: 'You are a *god,* and never have I heard anything more divine.'"[1]

* * *

Klossowski's experience lies here, more or less: in a

world where reigns an evil genius who has not found his god, or who might just as well pass himself off as God, or who might even be God himself. Such a world is neither Heaven nor Hell, nor limbo; it is, quite simply, our own world. That is, a world that would be the same as ours except for the fact that, indeed, it is the same. In this imperceptible divergence of the Same, an endless movement finds it place of birth. This movement is utterly foreign to dialectics; for it concerns not the test of contradiction, nor the game of identity at first affirmed then denied. The equation A = A is animated by an internal, unending movement which separates each of the two terms from its own identity and refers the one to the other by the game (the force and treachery) of this very separation. With the result that no truth can be engendered by this affirmation; however, a space of danger here begins to open up, in which the arguments, fables and booby-trapped, alluring ruses of Klossowski will find their language. A language which for us is as essential as that of Blanchot and Bataille, since in its turn it teaches us how the gravest of thought must find its enlightened lightness outside of dialectics.

In reality, neither God nor Satan ever appear in this space—a strict absence which is also their interweaving. But neither of the two is ever named, perhaps because it is they who invoke, rather than being invoked. This is a narrow, numinous region where all figures are the sign of something. Here one passes through the paradoxical space of real presence—a presence

[1] Italics are mine (*demon, I myself* and *god*). The text is from Nietzsche's *Gay Science* (trans. W. Kaufmann), as quoted in *Un si Funeste Désir,* an important collection which contains some very profound pages on Nietzsche and makes possible an entire rereading of Klossowski's work.

which is only real in so much as God has absented himself from the world, leaving behind only a trace and a void, so that the reality of this presence is the absence in which it resides, and in which it unrealizes itself through transubstantiation. *Numen quod habitat simulacro.*

This is why Klossowski hardly approves of Claudel's and Du Bos's summoning Gide to convert; he well knows that those who put God at one end and the Devil at the other (a god of bone against a devil of flesh) were mistaken, and that Gide was closer to being right when by turns he would come near and steal away, playing the devil's simulacrum at the behest of others, but not knowing, in so doing, whether he was serving as the devil's toy, object and tool, or whether he was not as well the chosen man of an attentive, crafty god. It is perhaps of salvation's essence that it is not announced by signs but takes place in the profound depths of simulacra.

And since all the figures that Klossowski sketches and sets in motion inside his language are simulacra, it is necessary that we understand this word in terms of the resonance that we may now confer upon it: vain image (as opposed to reality); the representation of something (in which this thing delegates itself and is manifested, but also withdraws and in a sense is hidden); a lie which leads one to take one sign for another;[2] a sign of the presence of a deity (and the reciprocal possibility of taking this sign as its opposite); the simultaneous irruption of the Same and the Other ("to simulate" originally meant "to come together"). Thus is formed the wondrously rich constellation so

---

[2] Marmontel said admirably: "Simulating would express the lies of feeling and thought" (*Oeuvres*, vol. X, p. 431).

characteristic of Klossowski: simulacrum, similitude, simultaneity, simulation and dissimulation.

* * *

For linguists, a sign possesses its meaning only by virtue of the play and sovereignty of all other signs. It has no autonomous, natural and immediate relationship with what it signifies. It is valid not only through its context, but also by means of a virtual reach which extends like a dotted line on the same plane as it: by virtue of this ensemble of all the signifiers which define a language at a given moment, it is forced to mean what it says. In the religious domain one often finds a sign entirely different in structure; what it says, it says by virtue of a profound belonging to an origin, by virtue of a consecration. There is not a single tree in the Scriptures, not a single living or dissicated plant which does not refer back to the tree of the Cross—or to the wood cut from the First Tree at the foot of which Adam succumbed. Such a figure breaks down into stages through moving forms, which gives it that strange, twofold property of designating no meaning in particular but of referring back to a model (to a simple of which it is supposed to be the double, but which takes it back within itself as its own diffraction and transitory duplication) and being bound to the history of a manifestation that is never completed; within this history the sign may always be deferred to some new episode where a simpler simple, an earlier model (though later in Revelations) will appear, giving it an entirely opposite meaning; thus the tree of the Fall one day becomes what it has always been, the tree of the Reconciliation. A sign of this sort is at once prophetic and ironic: hanging entirely from a future that it repeats in advance, and which will repeat *it* in turn, in broad daylight. It says this, then that, or rather it already said, without our knowing, both this and that. In its essence it is a simulacrum, saying everything simultaneously and ceaselessly simulating something other than that which it says. It presents an image that depends on a forever receding truth—*Fabula*; and it binds in its form, as in an enigma, the avatars of the light that will come to it—*Fatum*. Fabula and Fatum, both sending us back to the first utterance from which they spring, that root which the Latins understood as word, and in which the Greeks saw the greatest essence of luminous visibility.

Clearly it is necessary to make a rigorous distinction between signs and simulacra. They do not at all involve the same experience, even though they may happen at times to overlap. For the simulacrum does not determine a meaning; it belongs to the realm of appearance, in the explosion of time: Noontide illumination and eternal recurrence. Perhaps the Greek religion knew nothing but simulacra. First the Sophists, then the Stoics and the Epicureans wanted to read these simulacra as signs—a rather belated reading, in which the Greek gods were effaced. Christian exegesis, which is of Alexandrian birth, has inherited this mode of interpretation.

In the great detour that is our own current experience, whereby we attempt to sidestep all the Alexandrianism of our culture, Klossowski is the one who, from the bottom of the Christian experience, has rediscovered the marvels and depths of the simulacrum, beyond the games of yesterday: those of sense and non-sense, of signifier and signified, of symbol and sign. It is this, no doubt, which gives his work its religious, solar aspect once one grasps in it the Nietzschean interplay of Dionysius and Christ (since they are each, as Nietzsche saw, a simulacrum of the other).

The realm of simulacra, in Klossowski's oeuvre, conforms to a precise set of rules. The reversal of situations takes place in the moment, the inversion of for and against being effected in an almost detective-genre fashion (the good become bad, the dead come back to life, rivals turn out to be accomplices, executioners are subtle saviors, encounters are prepared long beforehand, the most banal statements are endowed with double-meanings). Each reversal seems to be on the road to an epiphany; but in fact each discovery only makes the enigma more profound, increases the uncertainty, and never reveals an element except to conceal the relationship existing among all the other elements. But what is most unusual and difficult in all this, is that the simulacra are neither things nor clues, nor those beautiful motionless forms that were the Greek statues. Here the simulacra are human beings.

Klossowski's world is sparing of objects; moreover, they form only meager connections between the men whose doubles and as it were precarious intervals they constitute: portraits, photographs, stereoscopic views, signatures on checks, open corsets that are like the empty but still rigid shells of a figure. On the other hand, the Simulacra-Men abound: still few in number in *Roberte*, they multiply in *La Révocation* and especially in *Le Souffleur*, so much so, in fact, that this latter text, nearly stripped of all setting and materiality that might bring fixed signs to bear on interpretation, no longer consists of much more than a sequential joining of dialogues. The point is that humans are simulacra much more vertiginous than the painted faces of deities. They are perfectly ambiguous beings because they speak, make gestures, communicate by winks of the eyes, move their fingers and appear suddenly in windows like semaphores (is it to send signs or to give the impression of doing so while in fact they are only making simulacra of signs?).

With such characters as these, one is dealing not with the profound, continuous beings of reminiscence, but with beings consigned, like those of Nietzsche, to a profound forgetfulness, to that oblivion which makes possible, in "re-collection," the sudden appearance of the Same. Everything in them is breaking apart, bursting, presenting itself and then withdrawing in the same instant; they might well be living or dead, it matters little; oblivion in them oversees the Identical. They signify nothing; they simulate themselves: Vittorio and von A., uncle Florence and the monstrous husband, Théodore who is K., and especially Roberte who simulates Roberte in the minute, insuperable distance through which Roberte is such as she is, *this* evening (cf. *Roberte ce soir*).

* * *

All these simulacra-figures pivot in place: rakes become inquisitors, seminarians become Nazi officers, the confused persecutors of Théodore Lacase find themselves in a friendly semicircle around the bed of K. These sudden twists only come about by means of the play of "alternators" of experience. These alternators are, in Klossowski's novels, the sole peripeties—but in the literal sense of the word: that which ensures the detour and return. Thus: the test-provocation (the stone of truth which is at the same time the temptation of the worst: the fresco of the *Vocation*, or the sacrilegious task assigned by von A.); the specious inquisition (censors who present themselves as former rakes, like Malagrida or the psychiatrist with dubious intentions); the two-sided conspiracy (the "resistance" network which executes Dr. Rodin). But most of all the two great configurations which cause appearance to alternated are hospitality and the theatre: two structures which stand face to face with each other in reverse symmetry.

The host (a word which in French—*hôte*—already whirls about its interior axis, meaning both the thing and its complement, host and guest), the host offers what he possesses, for he can only possess what he proposes—which is there before his eyes and is for everyone. He is, to use the wonderfully ambiguous word, *regardant*.[3] Surreptitiously and with avarice, this giving regard sets aside its own portion of pleasure and confiscates by sovereign authority one aspect of things which *regards* only it. But this regard has the power to absent itself, to leave the place it occupies empty and to offer instead what it envelops with its avidity. Thus its gift is the simulacrum of an offering, as soon as it only preserves the feeble, distant silhouette, the visible simulacrum of what it gives. In *Le Souffleur* the theatre takes the place of this giving "regard," such as it reigned in *Roberte* and *La Révocation*. The theatre imposes on Roberte the role of Roberte; that is, it tends to reduce the interior distance which opened up in the simulacrum (under the effect of the giving regard), and to make the double of Roberte, separated from Roberte by Théodore (perhaps K.), be inhabited by Roberte herself. But if Roberte plays her role with natural ease (which comes to her at least as if on cue), it is no longer but a simulacrum of theatre; and if Roberte on the other hand stumbles through her text, it is Roberte-Roberte who slips away beneath a pseudo-actress (and who is a poor actress in as much as she is not an actress but Roberte). That is why this role can

---

[3] The French *regardant*, as discussed here by the author, means "particular, careful, punctilious" as well as "stingy, close-fisted"; it also, as a noun, means "onlooker," and since Foucault is playing on all these meanings, I have left it in the original French. (Translator's note.)

only be played by a simulacrum of Roberte who resembles her so much that Roberte herself might well be this simulacrum herself. It is thus necessary that Roberte have two existences, or that there be two Robertes with one existence; she must be a pure simulacrum of herself. In the *regard*, it is the *Regardant* who is made double (and until death); on the stage of the false theatre, it is the *la Regardée* (the woman seen) who undergoes an irreparable ontological split.[4]

Yet behind this whole game of alternating experiences in which the simulacra flicker, is there some absolute Operator who is thereby sending out enigmatic signs? In *La Vocation Suspendue* it seems that all the simulacra and their alternations are organized around a greater invocation which makes itself heard within them or which, perhaps, just as well remains mute. In the subsequent texts, this imperceptible but "invoking" God has been replaced by two visible figures, or rather two series of figures who are, in their relation to the simulacra, at once with both feet on the ground and in perfect disequilibrium—both dividing, and divided, in two. At one end, the dynasty of monstrous characters, at the borderline of life and death: the professor Octave, or that "old master" that one finds at the beginning of *Le Souffleur* controlling the shuntings at a suburban train station, in a vast, glazed hall before or after life. But does this "operator" really intervene? How does he tie the plot together? Who is he, really? Is he the Master, Roberte's uncle (the one with two faces), Dr. Rodin (the one who dies and is resuscitated), the lover of stereoscopic spectacles, the chiropractor (who massages and works on bodies), K. (who steals the

---

[4] Here one encounters again—though as a pure form, in the stripped-down game of the simulacrum—the problem of real presence and of transubstantiation.

works and perhaps the wives of others when he's not giving away his own wife), or Théodore Lacase (who makes Roberte act)? Or is he Roberte's husband? A vast genealogy runs from the Almighty to the one crucified in the simulacrum that he is (since he, who is K., says "I" when Théodore speaks). But at the other end, Roberte herself is the great operatrix of the simulacra. Tirelessly, with her hands, her long, beautiful hands, she caresses shoulders and heads of hair, arouses desires, recalls former lovers, gives herself to soldiers or seeks out hidden miseries. It is without question she who diffracts her husband in all the monstrous or lamentable characters in which he scatters himself. She is legion. Not the one who always says no, but, inversely, the one who forever says yes. A forked yes which gives rise to that interspace where everyone stands beside himself. Let us not say Roberte-the-Devil and Théodore-God; let us say, rather, that the one is the simulacrum of God (the same as God, hence the Devil), and that the other is the simulacrum of Satan (the same as the Evil One, hence God). But the one is the Insulted-Inquisitor (laughable seeker of signs, obstinate and always disappointed interpreter—for there are no signs, only simulacra), while the other is the Holy-Sorceress (forever on her way to a Sabbath where her desire invokes human beings in vain, for there are never any humans, only simulacra). It is in the nature of simulacra not to tolerate either that exegesis which believes in signs or that virtue which loves humanity.

Catholics scrutinize signs. Calvinists have no trust at all in them, because they only believe in the election of souls. But what if we were neither signs nor souls, but merely the same as ourselves (neither visible sons of our works, nor predestined), and thereby torn apart in the discrete distance of the simulacrum? Well, the point is that the signs and destiny of man supposedly no longer have a common ground; the point is that the Edict of Nantes supposedly was revoked; that we are henceforth in the void left behind by the division of Christian theology;[5] and that on this deserted earth (which might indeed be rich from this abandonment) we can turn our ears to the words of Hölderlin: "*Zeichen sind wir, bedeutungslos,*" and perhaps still beyond, to all those great and fleeting simulacra that made the gods sparkle in the rising sun or shine like great silver arches in the heart of the night.

This is why *Le Bain de Diane* is probably, of all of Klossowski's texts, the one closest to this dazzling—but to us gloomy—light, from which the simulacra come to us. In this exegesis of a legend we find a configuration similar to the one that gives order to his other narratives, as though they all had their great mythical model therein: a proclamatory fresco as in *La Vocation*; Actaeon is Artemis's nephew, as is Antoine to Roberte; Dionysius is Actaeon's uncle and the old master of drunkenness, of anarchy, of death forever revived, of perpetual theophany; Diana is divided in two by her own desire, Actaeon metamorphosed at once by his desire and by that of Artemis. And yet, in this text devoted to an interpretation of a remote legend and a myth of distance (man chastised for having attempted to approach the naked goddess) the offering is as close as can be. There the bodies are young, beautiful, whole; they flee toward one another with all certainty.

---

[5] When Roberte the Calvinist, in order to save a man, violates a tabernacle in which real presence is *not* hidden, she is suddenly seized, through that miniscule temple, by two hands, which are her own: in the void of the sign and of the artwork, the simulacrum of the doubled Roberte triumphs.

The simulacrum still presents itself in its sparkling freshness, without resorting to the enigma of signs. There, phantasms are the welcome of appearance in the light of origin. But this origin is one that by its own movement recedes into an inaccessible remoteness. Diana at her bath, the goddess stealing away into the water at the moment in which she offers herself to the gaze, is not only the turning away of the Greek gods; it is the moment in which the intact unity of the divine "reflects its divinity in a virgin body," and thereby doubles into a demon who makes her, at a distance from herself, appear chaste and at the same time offers her to the violence of the Goat. And when divinity ceases to shine in the clearings only to split in two in the appearance where it succumbs while vindicating itself, it leaves the space of myth and enters the time of theologians. The desirable trace of the gods withdraws (and perhaps is lost) in the tabernacle and the ambiguous play of signs.

At this point the pure word of myth ceases to be possible. How can one henceforth transcribe into a language such as ours the lost but insistent order of simulacra? The word perforce must be impure, which draws such shades toward the light and wants to give back to all simulacra, beyond the river, something like a visible body, a sign or a being. *Tam dira cupido*. It is this desire which the goddess placed in Actaeon's heart at the moment of metamorphosis and death: if you can describe the nudity of Diana, you are welcome to do so.

Klossowski's language is the prose of Actaeon: the transgressive word. Is not every word so, when it must deal with silence? Gide and many others with him wanted to transcribe an impure silence into a pure language, no doubt not seeing that such a word only possesses its silence from a much deeper silence that it does not name and which speaks in it and in spite of it—thus rendering it confused and impure.[6] We now know, thanks to Bataille and Blanchot, that language owes its power of transgression to an inverse relationship, that existing between an impure word and a pure silence, and that it is in the indefinitely travelled space of this impurity that the word may address such a silence. For Bataille, writing is a consecration undone: a transubstantiation ritualized in reverse where real presence becomes again a recumbent body and finds itself led back to silence in an act of vomiting. Blanchot's language addresses death: not in order to triumph over it in words of glory, but so as to remain in that orphic dimension where song, made possible and necessary by death, can never look at death face to face nor render it visible: thus he speaks to it and of it in an impossibility that relegates him to an infinity of murmurs.

Klossowski knows these forms of transgression well. But he recaptures them in a movement that is entirely his own: he treats his own language like a simulacrum. *La Vocation Suspendue* is a simulated commentary on a story that is itself a simulacrum, since it does not exist or rather it lies entirely within the commentary made on it. As a result, in a single layer of language there opens up that inner distance of identity that enables the commentary on an inaccessible work to exist in the very presence of the work and enables the work to slip away inside this commentary, which is nevertheless its only form of existence: the mystery of real presence and the enigma of the Same. The Roberte trilogy is treated differently, at least in appearance—journal fragments, scenes with dialogues, long exchanges that

---

[6] On the word and purity, cf. *Un si Funeste Désir*, pp. 123-125.

seem to tilt the word toward the currency of an immediate language without overview. But among these three texts a complex relationship is established. *Roberte ce Soir* already exists inside the text itself, since the text recounts Roberte's decision of reproof against one of the novel's episodes. But this first narrative also exists in the second, which contests it from within through Roberte's journal, and later in the third, where one sees its theatrical representation being prepared, a representation which escapes into the very text of the *Souffleur*, where Roberte, called upon to give life to Roberte through her identical presence, splits apart into an irreducible gap. At the same time, the narrator of the first story, Antoine, breaks up, in the second, between Roberte and Octave, then is scattered in the multiplicity of the *Souffleur*, where the one speaking is, without one's being able to determine for certain, either Théodore Lacase or K., his double—who passes himself off as him, wants to take credit for his books and finally finds himself in his place—or even the Old Man, who presides over the shuntings and remains the invisible "breather" (Souffleur) of all this language. A breather already dead, breather and breathed—perhaps Octave speaking yet again beyond death?

It's neither the ones nor the others, probably, but rather this overlapping of voices that "breathe" one another, insinuating their words into the other's speech and animating him with a movement, a "pneuma" that is not his own—but also breathing in the sense of a breath, an *expiration* that extinguishes the light of a candle; and lastly breathing *(soufflant)* in the specifically French sense of cheating or trickery, where one seizes upon something destined for another (taking his place, his role, his situation, his wife). Thus, as

Klossowski's language recuperates itself, looming over what it has just said in the swirl of a new narration (and there are three, just as there are three turns in the spiral staircase adorning the cover of *Le Souffleur*), the speaking subject is dispersed into various voices that "breathe" and "trick" one another, suggest, extinguish and replace one another—scattering the act of writing and the writer himself into the distance of the simulacrum in which he loses himself, breathes and lives.

As a rule, when an author speaks of himself as an author, it is in the vein of the "diaristic" confession that tells of everyday truths—an impure truth in a spare, pure language. In this recovery of his own language, this retreat that inclines toward no intimacy, Klossowski invents a space of the simulacrum that is without doubt the contemporary, but still hidden, place of literature. Klossowski writes a work, one of those rare works which discover: in it, one sees that the existence of literature concerns neither humans nor signs, but this space of the double, this hollow of the simulacrum where Christianity has fallen under the spell of Demon, and where the Greeks once feared the gleaming presence of the gods with their arrows. It is the distance and proximity of the Same where the rest of us, now, encounter our only language.

The Baphomet

To Michel Foucault

Prologue

Valentine de Saint-Vit, Lady of Palençay, whose lands abutted those of the Commandery of the Temple, had long cast a covetous eye on that prosperous domain. Her paternal great-uncle Jean, fulfilling a vow upon his return from the last Crusade, had granted two-thirds of his lands to the Order of the Temple, all the more readily as he had no direct descendant. The terms of the gift stipulated that the Brethren knights should assume the defense of the estate of Saint-Vit, which was bequeathed to his nieces, at that time called de Palençay; for the hundred or more years in which the Templars occupied the *dominant* fief, which they cultivated, enlarged and fortified with their own hands, all the adjacent lands of the neighboring estate came under the jurisdiction of the Commander. Now the Lord of Palençay, like his father-in-law before him, had never troubled to contest this privilege in his own behalf, having never resided in this dotal estate.

5

After the death of her husband, having returned there herself, Madame de Palençay grew impatient with the constraints of the protection which the Temple extended, to her mind abusively, over her lands. Married at age fifteen to Hugues de Palençay, she bore him no children. He was killed at Courtray. Finding herself a widow in charge of vast properties, she had no intention of remarrying. She was an attractive girl with a pleasant face, but was dry, cold and miserly. And if in the meantime she had adopted her pupil and nephew, the very young Lord of Beauséant, an orphan endowed with vast domains, here too it was merely to secure his estate for herself.

Having contacts at the Court, Madame de Palençay was one of the few people in the kingdom to guess King Philip's designs concerning the Order of the Temple. In the mad hope of recovering her ancestor's bequest—since in fact the Order of the Knights of St. John the Hospitaler, rivals of the Temple, stood the better chance of reaping this sacred possession of the Church—Madame de Palençay approached Guillaume de Nogaret with the intention of negotiating its eventual secularization. This sinister advisor of Philip at once understood the advantages to be gained from this woman, whose taste for lucre predisposed her to any and all endeavor. He falsely promised her that the lands would be reassigned to her in the event of the sequestration of the possessions of the Temple or else repurchased from the funds of the Commandery of Saint-Vit, provided that she managed to furnish him with overwhelming proof against the Temple regarding the morality of the Order, such as would support the investigation that was to follow.

When Madame de Palençay thus became certain of the main accusations to be brought against the

Brethren knights, she turned her attentions to her nephew Ogier. No affection bound her to this beautiful child of fourteen years—the usufruct of the Beauséant estate alone dictated the care she had visibly invested in his education. But as soon as she understood that in her attempt to attain her chimerical ends, much could depend on her pupil, she began to see him in an unforeseen light: thus absorbed as she was by the singular concern for her own self-interest, the chosen means to such ends kindled not a belated tenderness but vice in this perfectly insensitive nature. Since she had but a vague conception of that monstrosity which in the eyes of the times seemed to derive as much from sorcery as from lechery, she did not want to act before first consulting the one of her nephew's two tutors whom she preferred. The first, a Burgundian clergyman and chaplain of Palençay, later asserted that the second had been the cause of all the woe that followed. The latter (who some claimed was German and called Wallhauser, while others claimed was a Sicilian named Fra Sylvano) was versed as much in astrology as in medicinal botany, and had won the blind confidence of Madame de Palençay not only through predictions of his own that had come true, but also through operations that demonstrated the efficacy of his knowledge: they said that from afar he was capable of re-creating in the minds of others the image of a person he immersed in sleep; having subjected his pupil to such experiments, he no doubt exercised an irresistible influence over the young Ogier.

For his aunt and tutor—whom some might have deemed still desirable although she had passed her fortieth year—the young Lord of Beauséant felt a murky passion dictated by his newly awakened senses, which his shyness allowed him to express only in the guise of an unwavering obedience and devotion.

Madame de Palençay's lack of sympathy for her nephew might have been confused, in the eyes of the latter, with the kind of severity exacted by decorum in the customs of those hard times: when she was informed of the highly uncommon seductiveness that this child was capable of exerting over other men, according to Fra Sylvano himself, and since such was the means suggested by the infamous Nogaret, she decided that the time had come to be less distant and more kindly, in the hope that the young boy, naively prey to her flattering caresses, would become overwrought in his amorous zeal and unwittingly assume the behavior to be prescribed to him.

It was also said that the astrologer had predicted to Madame de Palençay that her nephew would never reach manhood and that she herself would change sex. She passionately hoped that the first prediction would come true and interpreted the second to mean that one day she would find herself so powerful in her fortunes as to discourage her brothers-in-law ever from setting themselves against her. When these predictions in fact came true, she was no longer in a position to verify them.

Sylvano was clever enough to dissuade her at first from pursuing such an outcome. "You must know, Madame," he said to her, "that every prophet is always an impostor. Everything he says in a figurative sense will be interpreted to the letter by ambition; that is why refusing to take his words literally makes a prophet of an impostor."

In this late period of the Holy Order—having become in its prosperity the interest-free lender, both itinerant and sedentary, as well as the treasurer of kings—the Brethren knights, besides having at their disposal squires and lay Brethren subject to monastic law, had permission to enlist the services of young laic nobles for their personal attendance, hunting and travelling; so that, as contrary as this practice might be to the primitive statutes of the Order, the institution of pages was gradually introduced into many a commandery.

Sir Jacques de Molay, Grand Master of the Temple, did not trouble to forbid it: for once these young people—who were received in their twelfth or thirteenth year—reached the age of becoming squires, they either became postulants and took vows and thus completed the requisite number of knights of the Temple, or they re-entered the world. Even so, by virtue of the bonds established between the Brethren knights and their pages, a spiritual solidarity was created between the Order and many a great feudatory family. Upon admission, the lay adolescents swore on their honor never to disclose under any circumstances anything they happened to witness inside the Brotherhood.

The Commander of Saint-Vit, although he could have easily suppressed this practice in his fortress, managed to tolerate it. A man of modest origins and strict morals, he did not take it upon himself to oppose the greatest lords among his Brethren—whether for reasons of timidity, politics, or simple probity— claiming the pretext that he himself merely preferred not to benefit from this practice; on the other hand, he awaited the opportunity of a reform: if ever a scandal should occur of the sort that according to rumor was already afoot, it was better to ascribe it to this practice extraneous to the monastic life, rather than to cast any more suspicion on the primitive statutes of the Holy Order.

In 1307, a few weeks before Philip ordered the arrest of the Templars throughout his kingdom, an event of trivial origin brought discord into the bosom of the Commandery of Saint-Vit.

The Commander noticed that for two days Brother Guy, Lord of Malvoisie, had appeared neither at offices nor at meals, and as he was surprised to discover that the aforesaid Brother knight had not requested permission to confine himself to his cell, due to some indisposition or other reason, and that none among the Brethren knights knew of or wished to clarify the misconduct of the aforesaid knight, after vespers on the third day two lay Brethren came to him and gave the following account: At the beginning of the week, they began, the said Brother de Malvoisie and Brother Lahire de Champsceaux had met in the refectory of the lay Brethren to play chess, and it soon appeared to the witnesses that, as far as they could follow the exchange between said knights, keeping to the background, the game's stakes were not some prized object or sum of money, but the very person of the young Ogier, Lord of Beauséant, enlisted in the services of Brother Lahire. The latter, finding himself defeated, was heard to declare to the victorious knight that in good and due form he was relinquishing his page to him.

The next day the young Lord Ogier was tardy in presenting himself to his new master. Brother de Malvoisie, put out that the boy had come neither by prime nor by sext, betook himself to Brother Lahire and began to accuse him of having conjured away his prize. Brother Lahire tried to calm him, but seeing him take so seriously an affair in itself so frivolous, he

10

gently reproached him that so fierce a rage could prevent him from participating in the offices of the evening before and in communal meals. But Brother de Malvoisie went further still, asserting that during a recent collation Lord Ogier had poured him a sleeping potion at the instigation of Brother Lahire; no doubt since the latter deemed him unworthy of sponsoring the young Beauséant to the rank of squire! While he persisted in demanding satisfaction for this insult—they continued—several knights, drawn by his cries and stamping feet, emerged from the neighboring cells and tried to intervene. Brother de Malvoisie withdrew at once; however, Brother de Champsceaux asked one man after another what had happened to the Lord of Beauséant in the meantime; for he said he did not doubt that if the child had had any aversion to taking part in a prank of so little consequence he would not have failed to tell him so; afterward, when the search for him in the three enceintes proved fruitless, the aforementioned Brother Lahire had his horse saddled shortly after vespers; since then, neither he nor his squire had come back to the fortress.

The curfew bell had just sounded when a third lay brother urgently requested an audience with the Commander at that late hour, and he declared that two days before the dispute, shortly after the game of chess, Brother de Malvoisie, having addressed the young Lord of Beauséant in the passageway, ordered him to follow him into his cell. The aforementioned Beauséant, who at that time still wore the black and white habit of the pages of the Temple, dared to retort to the said Brother knight that he was not in his services, that he himself descended from a higher lineage than said Brother knight, and that never would a Beauséant bend his knee to a Malvoisie if not

11

of his own free will; but that, knowing him to be a friend of his master, he would politely hasten to do his bidding at any time if the Brother knight would ask him courteously. The lay Brother added that, deeming it prudent on his part to withdraw—for fear that the knight would take him as a witness to the presumptuous words of Lord Ogier and summon his help in venting his anger on the child, as was his wont with the other valets and servants who gave him cause for displeasure—he saw Brother de Malvoisie cast furtive glances around him. Thus assured of being unobserved in the passageway of the cloister where the two of them stood, he bowed before the Lord of Beauséant and, having grasped the young boy's right hand, kissed it with an air of humility that the lay Brother deemed false, out of place as it was. Later, he said, the young Beauséant appeared in different parts of the fortress dressed in livery bearing the crest of Malvoisie; and he was among the cup-bearers at suppertime. Shortly after compline he reported to the gates of the third enceinte, under the pretext of bearing a message from Brother de Malvoisie to deliver outside; the officer of the guard, seeing him on horseback but without the Commander's safe-conduct, refused to lower the drawbridge. The men-at-arms forced him back to the first enceinte, where the young Beauséant suddenly and loudly cried out that he knew very well another way to leave this "Temple of Mammon where one was forced to serve two masters."

The Commander was a hard and limited man; but just as he remained ignorant of the teachings long passed on in the bosom of the Order so that he himself should abide solely by the letter of statutes, never delving into the secrets kept by certain groups of his Brethren, so he showed himself to be vigilant and clever in interpreting only outward signs whenever encountering a tacit infraction of the primitive Rule.

As soon as the Commander had completed his first inquest, although now and henceforth he knew from his own sources more than he let on—for in fact the petty jealousies aroused among the lay Brethren by the pages was to him a precious asset—in order to break the apparently concerted silence that surrounded him regarding these small details, he let it be known, at the end of the meal, that from that time forth the Brethren knights would no longer enjoy the privilege, theretofore improper, of maintaining pages inside his Commandery in addition to the squires and lay Brethren permitted them by the statutes. And, he continued, the young lay boys who were staying there and had not yet applied for ranks within the Order were to be dismissed.

As this decision elicited strong emotions among the Brethren knights, the Commander called together the Chapter and there, with the assistance of a Visitor of the Order, who had arrived in the meantime, he explained the deplorable incident that had just erupted and did not fail to lament the state of darkness in which he had been kept. Intimidated by the presence of the Visitor, come straightaway on behalf of the Grand Master to invest the Commander with full authority, the majority of the Brethren concurred with this resolution.

Assured of having the discipline of the statutes respected, the Commander, to the surprise of all, had the young Lord of Beauséant brought in, dressed in the livery of the house of Malvoisie, and summoned him to repeat what he had disclosed to him.

Sufficiently troubled to find himself in the presence of the Chapter, besides perceiving the Brother de

Malvoisie there in person, prostrated *in venia* at the feet of the Commander, the boy stammered with difficulty that he had never had any complaints whatsoever in the Brotherhood. Upon this, at a sign from the Commander, the buttocks of Lord Ogier were exhibited, where all could discern the marks of a recent flagellation. Murmurs rose among the side of the majority of Brethren, while those of the opposite side lowered their heads or turned away in silence.

The Visitor of the Order, deferentially addressing the young Lord of Beauséant, urged him not to hesitate to name the Brother guilty of or complicit in this act, and to state whether he himself suffered it by consent or by constraint, so that at the very least the Brother de Malvoisie could exculpate himself.

As Lord Ogier persisted in remaining silent, the Commander rose from his seat and approaching the young boy, took his hand and threaded a ring on his finger; then without a word he returned to his seat. Since all remained silent in astonishment and the young page, blushing with lowered eyes, remained immobile with one hand on his hip and not without a certain nonchalance, suddenly the Commander tossed a white robe at his feet. But since Lord Ogier did not take the trouble to pick it up, upon a sign from the Commander a man-at-arms approached, took it up and rested his hand on Beauséant's shoulder. The Commander inclined slowly forward, leaning on the arm of his chair. Lord Ogier bent his knee to the Commander and to the Visitor of the Order, and bowed to the Chapter. He was led away to the dungeon.

At this moment some thought that by putting the ring on his finger and tossing the white robe at his feet, the Commander implicitly meant tacitly to ac-

14

knowledge him at the rank of squire, and in this way extended his jurisdiction over the person of this young lay nobleman. Others conjectured that this gesture was a disapprobation addressed to those Brethren knights who allegedly in private recognized the Lord Beauséant at the rank of squire.

Then the Commander ordered the Brother de Malvoisie to rise and, as penance, confined him to his cell; firstly for having gambled with the person of a child during the course of a game, which he knew to be expressly forbidden; secondly for having flouted the forbearance of the Commandery in obliging the young lad to exchange the black habit of the pages of the Temple for the livery of the house of Malvoisie.

When these two persons had exited the Chapter, the Commander stated that the young Ogier was lying in one way or another, and that a secret bound him to either Brother de Malvoisie or Brother de Champsceaux. Beauséant, unable to leave the fortress, had come in person to see him at the hour of the curfew-bell, in order to protest the maltreatment of which he was allegedly the object. On that occasion he had asserted that the Brother de Malvoisie, having drawn him into his cell on some pretext, had administered him a thrashing as sudden as it was brutal and allowed him to leave his cell only when dressed in the livery of the house of the Brother knight; for this reason he begged to be sent back to Palençay. Since the boy shuddered at the thought of rejoining his would-be new master—or at least pretended to shudder—and likewise refused to take up service with Brother Lahire, continued the Commander, he himself had hidden him for the night in the cell next to his own, never dreaming of allowing him to leave the fortress after having voiced such grievous accusations. Moreover, he was sure whereof he spoke, having learned at dawn from a lay Brother that the said Lord of Beauséant had himself incited the former valet-at-arms of Brother de Malvoisie to flagellate him: the former valet, now squire to Brother de Bois-Guilbert, went about it so brutally that Lord Ogier, guessing a strong jealousy to be the cause, gave him a gift of a bracelet so that he should not continue to avenge himself in this manner. When the Brethren knights could not restrain themselves from laughter, the Commander specified that this valet-at-arms had been put into irons and observed that surely the spirit of evil breathed among the community if so unfortunate a detail could create such hilarity among the Brethren convened in the Chapter. The Commander added that he did not wish to probe any further into what had happened between the Lord of Beauséant and the two Brethren knights: all the same, he was not at all convinced by the alleged game of chess that the lay Brethren had naively denounced; but, since someone wanted to deceive him, he would deceive him in turn. It seemed to him that without a doubt treason had been prowling about inside the Commandery for the past few hours. For in fact, if the distressing events had taken place in the manner described by Lord Ogier, nothing would have prevented the latter from alerting him of it at the proper time, rather than deliberately leaving the fortress; and why did he choose to accede to the moods of the Brother de Malvoisie and then attempt to flee, rather than publicly request immediate leave? Was it for the same reason that reduced him to silence before the Chapter? Whether the child was innocent or guilty of mendacity, his purpose was to broadcast the imaginary—or quite possibly real— disturbances which the Brethren de Malvoisie and de

Champsceaux were fomenting. At last he added that the latter had been found in a pitiful state and, when calm was restored, he called in the Brother de Bois-Guilbert forthwith and begged him to tell the Chapter of the dangerous venture that had allowed him to bring the aforesaid Brother Knight back alive.

In few words the Brother de Bois-Guilbert recounted that during the night Brother Lahire's squire, returning alone to the fortress, had arrived more dead than alive: for, he declared out of breath, at Palençay the envoys of the King were torturing his master.

Bois-Guilbert added that having immediately surrounded the exits to the neighboring estate with some fifty Saracen auxiliaries (which the Commander retained with the greatest of secrecy), he himself charged Palençay with his squadron: finding the place without any notable means of defense on the periphery—for according to the stipulations of the bequest, the Commandery itself would see to its protection—he was at leisure to rout out and slaughter the bailiff's rabble and thus penetrate the manor house. Forced to use violence, he thought it wise to employ it to the full and swiftly; followed by a dozen men he ended up apprehending Madame de Palençay whom he found in secret council with two emissaries of Nogaret; seizing these two he tore Brother Lahire away from his torturers; sowing at the same time fire and terror throughout the outbuildings, he succeeded in bringing back, in various states of molestation, the noble lady and the respectable personages of the envoys of the King and all the others requested by the Commander, as many as his escort would permit him; as for those who had escaped alive, they would assuredly sound the alarm for a thousand leagues around. Sooner or later one could expect to see the Commandery of Saint-Vit attacked by the Seneschalsy of the bailiff. Having said this, Brother de Bois-Guilbert fell silent and wiped his brow.

Since the news of this nocturnal raid, which had been carried out unbeknownst to most of them, elicited much more consternation than approbation among the Brethren—notwithstanding the fact that it was a matter of life and death to one of their own, and that in their apparently stable tranquility they would never have suspected the Council of the King capable of setting ambushes for them so vile as to compel the Commander to act in such extreme fashion—the latter declared that he had acted wisely: that far from wishing openly to rebel against the power of the Throne, however bad were the rumors recounted by the Visitor on behalf of the Grand Master, he was indeed inviting the Brethren knights to profit from the delay granted by the circumstances to erase all traces of shame and malfeasance from the bosom of the Commandery and from the Temple as a whole. If in the near future the Holy Order were called before the Pope to account for its glorious past, they owed it to themselves beforehand to dispel all slanderous charges; for even if this deplorable incident hadn't got out of hand, the Council of the King showed itself ready to fabricate ever new surprises, and therefore all the more should they rejoice that the scandal was kept quiet in time, and in the bosom of the Commandery itself, according to the Rule of the Order, so that each could prepare himself with a clear conscience to appear before the justice of the Church, of which the knights remained the faultless defenders. Such being the will of the Grand Master, the Commander would see to its enforcement.

Having dismissed the Chapter, the Commander

detained the Visitor and the Seneschal so that they could hear Brother Lahire de Champsceaux's confession: barely able to walk, the latter was brought in, supported by two squires; for at Palençay the torturers had been at leisure to wreck his feet. The Commander asked what sort of confession they had to rend from him; the Brother answered that the royal emissary wanted to charge him with the kidnapping of the young Lord of Beauséant, of which Madame de Palençay had accused him; he denied as best he could that the child, whom he acknowledged having chosen as a page with the consent of the noble lady, was sequestered in the fortress; on the contrary, being worried himself at his disappearance, in all good faith he believed him to have returned to Palençay; indeed he himself would not have come had he not hoped to find him there. At this the royal emissary, having rejected such an allegation as false, had him tortured, with such insistence that at last the Brother knight, at the end of his tether, conceived the answer that the beginnings of an amorous tryst had drawn him to Palençay that day. Upon this semblance of a confession, they granted him a brief respite; he was dying of shame when Brother de Bois-Guilbert finally broke into the manor.

The Commander addressed a few words of comfort to him, exhorting him to repent and not to despair of divine mercy, all the more as in such extreme circumstances he had preferred to bring dishonor upon himself rather than give credence to a rumor defamatory to the Holy Order. And he gave the floor to the Visitor.

The latter asked Brother Lahire to report in all sincerity and confidence whether it was Madame de Palençay who proposed to him the services of her nephew; the Brother answered no. Before he admitted when and how he had met the boy, and for what reason he had become attached to him as a page, the Brother de Champsceaux, with many a sign of contrition and many a tear for the violent disturbances of which he was the cause, more than once accused himself of having brought misfortune down upon a head he still deemed innocent. He recounted that during this year's Holy Week a dream had come to him several nights in succession, although he was sleeping deeply: he saw himself hunting a stag in a forest, when the deer suddenly stopped fleeing and turned its head towards him:·although surrounded by trees, its face was that of a youth; assailed by hounds and soon skinned of its hide, the whole and entirely naked body of a young boy appeared. This dream he thought to have dreamt for one or two nights; thereafter the first visions occurred more rapidly than on the preceding nights, and the dream changed, it seemed to him: for the boy now ran off into a cave, now hid behind a thicket or a treetrunk, and slowly long branches began to emerge from behind the obstacle: stretching out his neck at last, with both his hands he thumbed his nose at him. Such was the dream. The Visitor of the Order interrupted him at this point, asking him if he experienced any pleasure when he had this kind of dream; Brother Lahire answered that it was a vexing dream, but that in having seen it so many times, he had acquired a taste for this vexation, in spite of the sadness it aroused. Continuing his account, he declared that when his turn had come to mount guard and survey the borders of the Palençay estate on horseback, when circling round the woods of Saint-Vit, he had suddenly come upon a richly dressed, very young man who appeared to be amusing himself in the woods and greeted him graciously; astounded to recognize the youth who many a time had flouted him in the aforementioned dreams—or so it seemed to him, for even though he couldn't describe his features precisely, still the same sensation came over him on the spot—the Brother knight asked him if he was a relation of Madame de Palençay or simply in her service; the said lad declared that he was called Ogier, Lord of Beauséant, presently in the tutelage of his aunt, the mistress of the place; while they chatted together, the Lord of Beauséant, approaching to caress and cajole Brother Lahire's charger, espied above one of his pasterns a nasty tumor that the fortress grooms despaired of healing; Lord Ogier suggested trying a plaster of his own preparation and the Brother knight consented; taking the Lord of Beauséant upon the crupper, the two of them made their way towards Palençay; during the ride, the young Beauséant showed that he knew a great deal; he seemed to know as much about the virtues of the plants that grew on the estate as about the different species of birds that he claimed to have raised in his aviary—so much so that the Brother knight was astonished. In time the plaster proved efficacious. During his visit to Palençay, desirous to render homage to the noble lady, he paid her many a compliment for being blessed with so learned a nephew, and neither did he refrain from intimating how fortunate he felt to have had at his disposal such a knowledgeable and gracious youth, who was the proper age to become a squire; he went so far as to make this request, which Madame de Palençay flatly refused on the grounds of the child's ill-health; this seemed specious to the Brother knight, who from the look of him knew him to be sturdy and in full bloom. It was not until the second interview that Madame de Palençay, not without a certain eagerness, gave in to him, adding two steeds to his stable which the child led with much skill on the day of his entry to the Commandery.

The Visitor of the Order asked the Brother knight if it was true that on some rides, instead of mounting his own horse, the Lord of Beauséant placed himself upon the crupper of Lahire's steed and at times (as the lay Brethren maintained) even set himself between the neck and withers of the steed and the saddle of his master. The Brother Lahire retorted that no position better suited the manner of conversation to which they were accustomed in their outings.

Upon this, the Commander had the Brother de Champsceaux led away by the Seneschal. Then, once alone with the Visitor of the Order, he declared that whatever came to pass in the near future, it would never be said that the glorious tree of the Holy Order bore bad fruit: these would be severed in advance. The Visitor betrayed his emotions somewhat; but having just granted him full authority on behalf of the Grand Master he fell silent, whether out of lassitude or because he deemed hopeless the position of the Holy Order, thus letting it be understood that in his fortress the Commander alone was responsible for the fate of his Brethren.

No sooner had the Visitor of the Order taken leave of the Commander than the Brother de Bois-Guilbert announced that the troops of the Seneschalsy had laid seige to the forests of Palençay and Saint-Vit; after advancing to a respectful distance from the walls of the Commandery, the bailiff's horsemen had withdrawn without presenting demands. Following the orders of the Commander, all available forces were in place along the enceintes, and a small number of

Brethren were patrolling beyond the moats. Otherwise, the day ended without further incident; for it later became known that throughout the kingdom the bailiff, forewarned as of the twenty-second of September of that year,[1] had received the order to remain in wait until the dawn of the thirteenth of October; so that the bailiff of B. not only did not disturb the Commandery of Palençay, he merely reported to the Commander that bands of looters had sacked the manor and kidnapped Madame de Palençay, leaving him no alternative but to occupy the lands in question. Thereupon the next day, the thirtieth of September, the Visitor of the Order returned to the Temple of Paris without incident.

The Commander nevertheless felt that—whatever the bailiff's game—the hours of the Commandery of Saint-Vit were numbered; consequently, after the curfew bell on this fifth day, so that this night should not be spent like the preceding one, he drew up his secret report intended for Sir Jacques de Molay, the Grand Master of the Temple; having finished it by the hour of matins, he set out for offices with a lightened heart.

For in fact, the evening of the previous day—when he had decided to keep the young Lord of Beauséant at his side—after putting the boy to sleep in the cell

[1]The investigations of isolated cases of Templars being prepared by the emissaries of the King's Council, cases such as that instituted by Madame de Palençay were, at this date, only part of the preliminary phase of the general operation envisaged by Philip against the Temple; if Brother Lahire had remained in the hands of his torturers, his confessions would only have been brought forward as evidence once the Templars had been arrested as a body, so that the Pope would be presented with a *fait accompli*.

next to his own almost an hour earlier, before getting some rest himself he decided to assure himself one last time that the child was not still awake, although all means of escape had been thwarted in advance; having found him on the contrary sleeping profoundly, he espied, attached to the child's unknotted belt, a bunch of rusted keys; he examined them and, taking posession of them, he called one of the lay Brethren and asked him to which locks of which doors of which closets, cabinets, chapels or cellars in the fortress their bits might correspond. Then, begging the Commander not to reveal his name if perchance he decided to use this information as evidence, the lay Brother recounted that during the day, before vespers, Brother de Malvoisie had been seen by the gardeners beside the so-called Tower of Meditation, at the western corner of the first and second enceinte. At that moment the Lord of Beauséant, still wearing the black habit of the pages of the Temple (which seemed to contradict previous testimony), joined him; both entered a small door at the base of the tower, on the side of the kitchen garden, where one goes down a few steps and enters the corridor of the middle cellar. But on the right one passes by a tiny door at once wide and very low: for years it had been locked and no one had ever thought of opening or forcing it. Now, before suppertime, the lay Brother was going to the cellar on his way to the casks when he was astonished to find this door ajar: curious to see where it led, he pushed it open, and advancing one step he discovered an ascending, narrow spiral staircase; he began to climb it, and after having twice circled round the central pillar, on about the fortieth step, he emerged onto a landing of flagstones of a vast circular oratory with high vaulting which let in daylight only through three loopholes on the side overlooking the moats; for on the side of the fortress, there was an interior window cut into the wall, through the stained glass of which one espied the open space of a gallery. In the oratory stood an altar, crowned with a crucifix stripped of the Savior's image; in front of the altar were two candelabra with half-consumed candles; on the altar was a tabernacle. As he distractedly climbed the steps, he stumbled on a hidden lever—at once the tabernacle opened and the gold head of a child appeared. A sparkling stone pupil in the enamel white of an eye followed the Brother's every move; when he stepped back a pace as the head's lips stirred in silence, the tabernacle closed forthwith. Terrified by this vision, he was about to rush towards the exit when he noticed, at the opposite end, a raised throne on which trailed a long robe, narrow at the shoulders and small as a choir boy's, but made of fine linen, embroidered with strange images in gold thread. The lay Brother suspected that what appeared before his eyes, the ornaments as well as the tabernacle's mechanism, had been shown by the Brother de Malvoisie to the young Lord of Beauséant, perhaps to prepare him for the rank of squire, in accordance with a ritual from which the lay Brethren were rigorously excluded; he swore to himself not to breathe a word of this to anyone, and already had one foot off the flagstones of the landing, beginning to descend the narrow staircase, when casting a last glance behind him towards the throne, he discerned between the back of the chair and the wall what he thought to be the hastily hidden pieces of the black habit of the pages of the Temple, as well as the surcoat and breeches; as he drew them from their hiding places, a glove fell to the floor; picking it up he noticed that in the hollow of one finger lay a ring; once extracted, it shone with a diamond engraved with the arms of the Temple. The lay Brother added that not daring to disturb this clothing he deemed it preferable to replace it as he had found it, pell-mell between the wall and the back of the chair. As for the ring . . . . But here the Commander silenced him with a gesture, having extended the palm of his hand: promptly the lay Brother placed his find there, surprised to be relieved of it so quickly; for although he had spoken in good faith, still the ring had seemed to keep him company.

Once the ring was in his hand, the Commander could no longer tell whether he was being guided by an irresistible power or acting of his own free will; for at once he reentered the neighboring cell and stealthfully approached the sleeping boy; gently raising Lord Ogier's left hand, he threaded the ring onto his third finger. Then he prudently removed it and, regaining his own cell, ordered the lay Brother to remove the white robe which the latter claimed to have found on the throne of the said place; and although he had his doubts about certain details that had been reported, he kept watch over the comings and goings around the Tower of Meditation. At last he decided to allow himself a few hours of sleep, but when he lay down one final question perplexed him: exactly what had Malvoisie and Beauséant been doing for them to flee so hastily when interrupted, neglecting to take anything with them, or to lock the door? Did they plan to return? He reviewed the circumstances of the accounts related by one lay Brother after another. It was merely a matter of small details—due allowance being made for the willful cunning of two or three individuals—yet the particulars began to agree less and less as the statements on the subject accumulated, forming a whole so incongruous that the less it appeared plausible, the more menacing it became. And if that night he restrained himself from waking Lord Ogier to interrogate him outright, just as he refused to go to the Tower of Meditation to see with his own eyes what all this was about, it was because he was afraid to look too closely, and afraid to act.

Then as he knelt before the crucifix and began to pray, turning his spirit to the mysteries of the Passion, vestiges of the images described by the lay Brother came back to him; and comparing to his own ring the smaller one he had placed before him, he gazed at the diamond of the latter so intently that he drifted off into a dream:

Alone, he was skirting the walls of the first enceinte on his way to the Tower of Meditation; he circled around there, but his touch could find no door; stumbling into gaping furrows he plunged into winding corridors so miserably narrow that he thought he would suffocate, although he was on the threshold of broader landings: standing at last, he came up against tiny doors with bolts so rusted that he broke the bits of his keys in them, while above him the vault vibrated with hurried footsteps: Malvoisie and Beauséant were fleeing in all haste, but he couldn't tell whether they were escaping outside or were running from one end of the gallery to the other; these deafening reverberations became mingled with the resonance of their voices, now near, now far away; like a girl, Beauséant shrieked with laughter; Malvoisie enjoined him to silence with a stifled cry.

Awake, he prayed to God to make him forget everything. Unable to force his knees to rest any longer on the flagstones, he left his cell and passed into the neighboring cell where the young traitor was sleeping like an angel; then, suddenly frightened that the child should see him standing there so wretched, he withdrew, stepping over the men-at-arms sprawled in the gallery; once again on the flagstones of his cell, he knelt; beating his breast and tearing his shirt, he scourged himself feebly before collapsing in exhaustion.

Sleep overcame him again: this time, indeed, he was on the right track: the door, the real one, located at last, was less low and much larger than the Brother had asserted; nimbly he bounded up the stairs which the Brother claimed led to the oratory; but here again the Brother had deceived him, for the stairway suddenly went straight up towards the upper ramparts where, in the calm of the night, Malvoisie, one hand on the young Beauséant's shoulder, the other indicating the Great Bear, was teaching his future squire the melody of the stars; the Commander was about to join them when he seemed to lose his footing . . . his vertigo vanished into shadowy space: his gnarled and icy hands seized at warm, youthful fingers; he had just fallen onto the very bed of the boy who, awakened and sweating with terror to see him thus—a tall shadow in his coat, stealing towards him—attempted with palms raised against this apparition to stop his blind advance. Yielding to the weight of the old giant, Lord Ogier did not offer the least resistance; he had expected it might be the Commander's turn, after his knights, since he had been hearing him prowl between his cell and his own for the past hour. And yet he was surprised that the Commander thought it necessary to seize his fingers and take them between his teeth, ready to bite them to the bone if the child began to struggle. No sooner did the Grand Master find himself flanked by the boy's feverish thighs than he pulled the covers over them; seeking the skin of the boyish chest, he slipped his forehead under his armpit and thus, while the heart of Lord Ogier beat to bursting against his ear, he tasted the sleep God had denied him.

Overcoming his distaste in confessing such weaknesses, the Commander noted all this, omitting no detail, in his missive to the Grand Master. For although he attributed the fact that he could fall so low in a single night to the sorcery of the ring, he nevertheless added that just as he judged others, he should likewise judge himself for having known this privilege and having suppressed it like a plague in his Commandery. The next morning he lifted the confinement imposed on Guy de Malvoisie the preceding day, called him into his cell, kissed him and begged his pardon for the severity with which he had treated him; thereupon in few words he exposed the perfidy with which Madame de Palençay had prepared her nephew to take advantage of the good faith of the Brethren knights; for this reason, as Madame de Palençay was suspect of libel, he had sequestered her person by virtue of the stipulations of the bequest which, in charging the Brethren knights with the defense of the Palençay domain, included her under the jurisdiction of the Holy Order. But as Beauséant stood accused of perjury and treason, and both were now under the jurisdiction of the Commandery, he personally laid the task of judging the aforesaid persons onto the shoulders of the Brother knight and his friends, who should find them guilty of the offenses and see to the execution of their punishment.

As Brother de Malvoisie, without changing expression, asked him in what place this exceptional court should sit in judgment, the Commander surrendered to the Brother knight the bunch of keys to the low door, saying that no doubt the time had come for the Tower of Meditation to earn its name.

Without further delay, the Brother de Malvoisie was led there under escort, and in the oratory he was more than a little surprised to find those intimates of his who, given short notice by their summons, did not dare to decline for fear of appearing to abandon him. Nevertheless Brother de Malvoisie begged the Commander to bring him the Brother Lahire de Champsceaux as well, with whom he wished to be reconciled and without whose help he declared himself incapable of passing judgment in this matter. Brother Lahire was thus in turn taken from his cell to the aforesaid place. When they were assembled, the Commander, having come himself to lay the white robe embroidered with gold on the seat of the throne, declared without further comment that he was sequestering them and would bring them provisions for as long as their deliberations lasted, for they must take the time necessary for the grave sentences that they had to pronounce; and that if perchance they decided on a sentence of death, it would be carried out by Saracen auxiliaries. Nevertheless he did not exclude the possibility that they would show leniency towards a child. As for Madame de Palençay, as much as she might seem a monster spewed from the depths of Hell, the Brethren should remember that they were Knights of the Temple, in whom Christian charity and the forgiving of trespasses should soften the warrior's wrath; or if nothing else, their courtesy as noblemen should bid them to respect a woman of rank, be she even a spy.

No sooner had he given the kiss of peace to each of them and thus taken leave of the Brethren judges, than he had the two prisoners, secretly kept apart, brought into chambers which led to the oratory either through the gallery behind the interior window or through the door that he was pleased to find behind the altar.

As for himself, he took up post behind an imperceptible chink in the vaulting through which he watched their movements.

— — — —

It seemed to him that Malvoisie and the seven others were only awaiting the moment of his departure to undertake at once the initiation of the neophyte, for as soon as he had glued his eye to the chink in the vaulting, the little he could see without at all grasping the meaning of the gestures, much less the meaning of their words, was none other than the peripeties and the rites of the first and second degrees, called the degrees of *Fear* and the *Shadow of Death,* which preceded the one entitled *O Death, where is your victory?* Thus he witnessed the enthroning of the victim, the young traitor whom the appointed judges had resolved to celebrate under the cover of his execution.

For in fact, as soon as they found themselves alone, they lit the candelabra: kneeling before the altar they intoned a chant.

At the first moment of silence, Lord Ogier is brought in by two Saracens. While these two withdraw, Malvoisie frees the child from his bonds, kisses his hands, leads him from one Brother to the next, and each kneels in homage to him.

Next Malvoisie directs Lord Ogier to the foot of the altar: there, while the Brethren knights remain prostrate with their faces to the flagstones, he strips the young Beauséant of the habit of the pages of the Temple; shining in his frail nudity by the light of the torches, the boy, on a sign from Malvoisie, ascends the stairs towards the open tabernacle in order to take hold of the object offering itself within. He extends his arms, then quickly draws back his hands—what does he seem to fear?

Behind him stands Malvoisie: holding a dagger to the boy's loins, he appears to be giving him a choice between two kinds of pain: once again the boy brings his hands towards the object, and having touched it lightly, once again he draws back: the iron point thus penetrates his flesh: as a shudder runs through his slender limbs, his whole body tightens and once again he plunges his hands into the tabernacle: and so he draws out the mysterious object, recently burning, now cold and light: the golden head perfectly reproduces his features: Malvoisie fits it to the child's head; and as he stands there, naked, the face alone veiled by its own image, enhanced, painted, shining, the knight leads him back to the base of the altar; here he stops him: and after pouring wine and oil on the wound he had just given him on the buttock, he smears the burn marks on his palms and his fingertips with an unguent, kneels and, putting an arm around his loins, his chin against the boy's stomach, kisses his navel; he stands up, unfolding over the child's head the white robe embroidered in gold, dresses him in it, the long, flared sleeves falling in long folds to his toes; taking him by the hand, he has him climb the steps to the throne, places him there and gathers his abundant hair into a mitre with lappets knotted beneath the chin; then clapping his hands, Malvoisie gives the other Brethren the signal for the major homage; one after another the seven knights ascend towards the mitred and masked young pontiff, naked under his robe. The boy offers at first his two palms to be kissed, but spreading his thighs he discloses his bountiful young

32

manhood; the knight kneels with his forehead buried in the youthful lap. Sweating under his golden mask, the mitred boy swoons, secured between the arms of the throne; then lowering his robe, he slaps the knight on both cheeks; the latter bows, goes back down and prostrates himself once more on the flagstones.

At this moment Malvoisie, who was standing next to the enthroned boy, returns to the center of the oratory: is it to procure a ritual accessory that the ceremony lacked? He is walking towards the altar when, from behind the tabernacle, he sees the Saracen auxiliaries surge forward in two rows; from the left and right they line up along the periphery of the oratory as the first two meet behind the throne. Others emerge from the opening in the flagstones, and stand motionless, prohibiting access.

Malvoisie casts a glance towards the interior window through the stained glass, where shadows are visible in the gallery. A rattling noise is heard.

Then, passing from one to the next, Malvoisie seems to whisper sinister tidings to the seven prostrate Brethren. Now he stands, while the others, as if forgetting the rite, begin to gesticulate wildly until, after a brief confabulation, upon a sign from Malvoisie towards the still closed window, the sound of a rattle once more resonates in the oratory.

Still seated on the throne, Lord Ogier, looking up towards the vault, saw a long rope with a running knot descend towards him.

Trembling like a leaf, tearing off the mitre and the gold mask and flinging them far from him on the flagstones, raising his hands up to his temples and tossing his long hair about, he began to run along the rounded walls of the oratory, out of his wits stumbling more than once on the fringe of his long robe soon stained and dirtied, hiding now behind the altar, now behind the throne where he had just reigned proudly. He was pulled away from there by the two heretofore stationary guards and thrown at Malvoisie's feet; clinging to the latter's knees, he implored him with both hands. Malvoisie drew back slowly. Silence fell. Lord Ogier, noting that the rope was drawn back up towards the vault, stood up, ashamed. Malvoisie then approached him and resting a hand on his long hair, whispered into his ear.

No doubt Beauséant thought that if he acquiesced to all their demands, his life would be spared. Temporarily calmed, he felt almost amused to see the rope redescending. Soon suffering a momentary strangulation, he allowed himself to be hoisted to the level of their faces. This reassured him further still. But soon they raised him up to the vault—and one could see him trying with his still free hands to find the pulley on which to grasp—then roughly let him fall into the Brethren's arms; in falling he let out such awful cries that the Brother Lahire de Champsceaux, no longer able to bear such odious charades, hurled himself at Malvoisie, his dagger raised; but he only wounded him in the shoulder. The overly sensitive Lahire was then garroted in the corner, where he remained sunken in shame and sorrow.

Beauséant, taken down and comforted by his initiators, changed his tactics. While the wine was circulating, seeing them begin to rave, he hastened to pour for them himself: they pretended not to tolerate that such a great lord should serve them, fed him a collation, and had already begun to argue which among them would warm himself that night at his side, when the interior window giving onto the oratory opened and Madame de Palençay appeared, impassive and haughty, shoved forward by Idris, the head of the Saracen auxiliaries. The Brethren lined up along the opposite side, leaving Ogier to face his aunt. Perhaps his aunt spoke a few words of blame to her nephew, for—or so it seemed to the Commander in his observation post— Ogier lowered his head and cried. Surprised by such contrition, they asked Ogier if this woman, his cruel relation, did not deserve to be punished. Entranced by the sight of Madame de Palençay, whom he had not expected to find there, Ogier suddenly answered that rather than see her perish he was ready to endure a thousand torments if, however, they could imagine anything worse than this, since they had already refused him death as too mild a punishment. Shocked by this sudden change and angered even more by such a fit of pride in this child who a moment before had been as indolent and docile as desired, Malvoisie declared that it was time for Madame de Palençay to leave her womanly state, and that to compensate her for having procured such a valiant squire for the Order, nothing prevented her from being herself proclaimed a Templar and being received among the Brethren; and Ogier, having demonstrated such perfect feminine aptitude, he continued, would henceforth belong to Idris, the Saracen chief.

Defenestrated and at once stripped naked, Madame de Palençay found herself hurriedly squeezed into a coat of mail; and thus, bending her knee before Malvoisie, Valentine de Saint-Vit was dubbed knight. Next they set her upright and—without concerning themselves in the least with her howlings or the grant she swore to make them if only they would allow her to end her days with the Ursulines—they laid bare her abdomen; Madame de Palençay, remembering Sylvano's words, understood that her destiny was about to be fulfilled to the letter; for if one is to believe the anonymous chronicler, a haughty little dragon sprang forth. "Is this then the reason Sir Hugues died without issue?"—Brother Malvoisie is said to have cried. And teasing this honorable ordinary with the point of his dagger, he drove her to the peak of frenzy.

At the interior window where he had taken Madame de Palençay's place next to the terrible Idris, Lord Ogier, the cord around his neck, stripped of his white robe, entirely naked, witnessed the dubbing of his aunt. Idris, who was holding him by the end of the rope, noticing that Beauséant could less and less conceal a boyish agitation, grazed his flanks with the hempen knot, whispering this warning into his ear: "Woe to you if you're not chaste!"

Dubbed at the cost of her honorable ordinary, Valentine de Saint-Vit cried out in rage; and then—had it not been written that he would never attain manhood?—an instant later, Beauséant was dangling in the void.

The Commander, disappointed that the first peripeties had not in the least modified his notion of human nature, had not waited to see the rest before leaving his secret post. He spent the remainder of his day in prayer in his chapel, and in confession he accused himself of impure glances, while on his order the door to the oratory in the Tower of Meditation was being walled up. The next day, leaving the Mass for the dead which he had celebrated, he passed his hand over the still damp limestone and breathed a sigh of relief.

The royal emissaries he had detained as hostages in his fortress were witness to this; for three days later he brought them to the secret chink in the vault, that they might have a glimpse of the place. They recoiled in horror. And after having given proof of the severity of the Holy Order towards its unworthy members, he continued to treat them humanely until the day when he himself made his surrender to the troops of the King.

I

"Tear yourself from this place of sorrow!" murmured the breeze that permeated his own swirls as he floated above the unrecognizable Island of the Cows.

The vast forests south of the capital, the hillsides sloping towards the northern ramparts, even the Tower of the Temple had vanished: not a single windmill's vane in this valley of the Seine, only a relief in stone as far as the eye could see, bristling with metallic carcasses all along both banks, a swarming blackness showing through the sulfurous haze.

The words he heard imparted a broader spiral to his expectation: "Is that you?" He unfurled himself to the beckoning of this familiar trembling in the air: he had recognized her, abandoning himself to the joy of having been recognized by her in turn:

"O breath of solace at the Vesperal hour when doubt besets our spirits! Tell me, how could so many plagues and wars not have overcome this greedy race? Will it continue to perpetuate itself for long? Many are

39

called and few are chosen, an ever variable number of
births depending on whether life down there is more
or less gentle or harsh, tranquil or murderous: does it
now reserve for me a new throng of breaths in wait?
Such chaos wastes my zeal! What can the Creator have
in mind? The stars withdraw in desperate flight from
this profusion of wasted souls! For as long as Judgment Day recedes from century to century, the older
souls stake out more recent ones, and merging by
affinity, they agree to obliterate their responsibilities
in each other, or in twos or threes; mutually compli-
cated, pretending to be an indissoluble whole, they
come and go through my fortress, defying my scrutiny
and reason! What lacerations there will be when they
resurrect! If indeed each must forever recover his dust,
his own, down there, to be judged for it here—as I
strive in vain to make them understand during their
detention, which it is my lot to guard!

Having thus spoken, he rose high above the towers
of Nôtre Dame. But the breeze carried him far from the
murmurs of that cursed site:

"For a long time have I awaited this weary and
bitter moment, I who never cease to be moved by your
great patience in teaching the expired breaths, O
Grand Master of the Temple! Nor have I wished to
disturb your faith in the task assigned you by the
Thrones and Dominions. But a cycle of events has
here run its course. The time has come at last to warn
you that the ranks of the elect are closed. Henceforth
humankind has changed in substance: it can be no
more damned than saved. Thus the endless pullula-
tion that you find so baffling. So heavy is the weight
of these expired souls that it upsets the equilibrium of
the spheres. This vast number of souls is forever
turning over on itself in vain. I would have you know

that whenever the breaths escape your vigilance and discover a being of the flesh, they infiltrate it not in twos or threes, as when they merge themselves, but in fives and sevens in a single uterus, eager to arrogate themselves an embryo upon which to discharge their former sins and recuperate new virtues: Most often it begins in the womb of some poor madwoman; a body too fragile is called upon to forge the apparent unity of a complex of seven souls and thus, a stormy, exuberant, intractable nature comes to suffer the tumult of so many breaths, exhaled so many times— differing in origin, age and lot—and even takes on their fortunes as its own! This body, sorely tried, is soon destroyed; its breath rises up here, divides itself according to its different components, which at once begin to quarrel, pursue each other, and finally disperse themselves in others more violent than they! This is why rapes and debauchery are redoubling, multiplying tenfold, one hundredfold in the lower world, and yet this still does not suffice to accommodate such travesties; and however much the births increase, the number of expired souls that want to be reborn will always exceed the number of babies born in both good years and bad. For this reason, rather than attempting this bastard solution, most expired souls prefer rapes and debaucheries on high, which sully your fortress. Until the day God deigns to create a new species, your task will only become more and more toilsome: the souls' turbulent anarchy, their adulteries, their incests in the circle assigned to you will only grow in size and number! For as soon as most of them no longer feel obliged to resurrect, God abandons them to their own judgment."

The breeze fell momentarily. The breath of the Grand Master lay still: "Is it really you who were speaking, bride of the Heavens? Theresa, where are you?"

Gunshots alternated with outcries, ululations, the ringing of bells; forthwith the grinding of teeth, sobbings and deafening jeers proceeded like high winds towards the air-hole that he himself had formed in the perplexing suspension in which the words of the breeze had left him. But already a whirlwind cavalcade of Brethren Breaths, banners unfurled, tracked down and collected this wave of exhaled breaths into a cumulus of thunderclouds that gilded the fires of the setting sun; then forming a vast funnel by their numerous and rapid maneuvers, the knights diverted them in torrents into the fortress's enceinte. The fortress sank its uncertain foundations deeper and raised the crowns of its five towers heavenward. To travellers and the peasants of neighboring hamlets, it looked like a majestic, blackened ruin: no one suspected what the slightest quivering of the ivy that had overrun it concealed, nor what was taking place within the apparently empty halls just a few steps from the ruminating livestock.

"What will you do with them all?" was whispered to him in the renewed silence.

The last of the Brethren knights had just crossed the drawbridge: Slowly, amidst the moaning effort of the postern's pulleys, the vast rectangle of planks resumed its vertical position. The sparkling water of the moat greeted the rising moon as though smiling. Three times the sounding of a horn reverberated in the inner courtyards.

But very near to his own breathing a mad, stifled laugh unfurled across the grasses of the dell.

Then, returning to him in a warmer flow:

"And now, Grand Master of the Temple, I beg your

1. *Malvoisie initiant le jeune Ogier aux secrets du temple.*

". . . Malvoisie, one hand on the young Beauseant's shoulder, the other indicating the Great Bear, was teaching his future squire the melody of the stars. . . ." (Page 28) assistance! Welcome me as you have just welcomed them! For I have excluded myself from the numbers of the elect and I have turned away from the face of God!"

At these words he fled, terrified. No doubt—while he was succumbing to the lure of the island which had vanished with the spent pyre of his agony—some breath, as baleful as its murmurs were sweet, had followed him to the edge of these banks, seeking to impose itself upon his sorrow: it imitated the inflexions of the saint whom at first he had thought to recognize. And, feeling himself overtaken, he cried:

"Never could one of the Blessed, if ever he so wished, lower his gaze from the face of God!"

"O presumptuous Doctors of the Church who declare us forever fixed within the almighty Good! If such is the end of our desire, the sight of it does not deprive us of our will as do the lower pleasures: He who fills me augments my consciousness of those who will never be allowed to see his face! O the unbearable happiness of the intelligence that God does not choose to shatter! In me God alone opposes God!"

The breeze that had borne these words swelled into such a squall that his own breath was cast down upon the ramparts of his fortress—the wind was intolerable there; howling in the foliage of the surrounding forest, it came back to beat the sides of the towers and whistle through the loopholes. This show of violence was in face nothing more than a polite request addressed to the master of the place; and although it could have entered at will, it waited for his consent. If only he had listened a moment longer to these arguments outside his enceinte, he would have relinquished forthwith the charge entrusted him by the Thrones and Dominions. It had to come inside his fortress to solicit him; for this was a question of canon law and obedience to the sound doctrine. Thus, pretending to stop his ears, he was swept through the watchtower and into a spiral staircase. The small door slammed behind him.

But this wooden door could even have been made of bronze and these walls hewn of diamond, still nothing which here served to separate or isolate was of any consequence: his own escape was but a gesture in response to another gesture and no other "outside," except intention, could prevail over this "inside"; in other words, no intention could help but be penetrated by another: here all intention was permeated by intentions. Only past intentions so intense as to wish the future prevailed over the others. What was thus the future if not a deliverance predicted in the past? Where else could predictions take root if not in the past? But what future was not the object of any prediction? From what celestial region emanated this breeze gusting back on itself through the ancient foliations of hope? As if it could not unreel the future without reeling up the past, prophesying like an obsolete servitude—thus, breathing from the depths of this very obsolescence, it drew the words out by the roots, showing there and then, deliverance . . . .

No longer did he doubt that it was she who had spoken to him. But judging that there were too many hostile emanations infesting the purlieus of his fortress not to throw such resonance intentionally into confusion, amplifying into a roar all that a contemplative soul had only murmured, the Grand Master, far from venturing to reflect on it, stood fast in his first impulse to anger.

Thus did he pass resolutely into the Chamber of the Bellows.

II

Although he had always felt a profound aversion to the instrumental mode which here offered itself as a means to inform the expired breaths, he told himself that he had been wrong to dismiss its spiritual efficacy on the basis of the devices' appearance, to the point of never making use of them. For if these devices seemed too exclusively to favor the physical accidents of informable substance, nonetheless, this itself was but a purely analogical reminder of the substance created imperfect but perfectible; these implements, by virture of their servile function, operated with all the more justice because he himself, a breath created and thus imperfect, could not raise himself to so sublime an impartiality as to dispense entirely with their service. Moreover, the instrumental mode was for the most part rectified by the presence of a sacred object which alone was fit to confer its emblematic character on the entire operation. Mechanically, these devices performed a ritual.

In the Chamber of the Bellows, also known as that of the *Bronze Serpent*, the Commander, the Visitor of the Order, and the Seneschal awaited him like so many columns whirling about themselves more or less slowly according to their respective ranks. At the back of the chamber, above an immense fireplace, was a cross—which instead of presenting the Savior's form retained only His crown of thorns and the four nails of His passion; there, two lay Brethren whose zealous whirlings resembled arms with rolled-up sleeves, had already made ready to seize the handles of a double bellows whose leather valves, inserted beneath the fireplace's hood like enormous testicles, concealed the duct; at the level of the hearth, on the dormant embers, lay a long and sinuous form of hollow metal, the *Bronze Serpent* of Moses which, it was said, Saladin had once given to the Grand Master Roncelin. Connected to the fireplace and aspirating the souls separated, discharged and gathered in the empty spaces of the tower next door, the double bellows expelled their first posthumous wailings over the hearthstone: as soon as the Bronze Serpent reached a state of incandescence, one of the laymen, equipped with tongs, attached its tail to the tube of the double bellows; thus under the harrowing cries of the separated souls, the incandescent snake unwound its coils in ever variable rings along which each expired breath was supposed to reveal or disguise what remained of its intention.

Whether he was the originator or simply the executor of this superstitious custom, the Commander took upon himself the responsibility for this manner of informing, to the indifference of the Grand Master, who cared little for it. For in fact, reinvested with his charge of Grand Master by the Thrones and Dominions, his own expired breath exercised within itself an immediate and secret mode of informing separated souls, of which he alone had the power. Now it so happened that having thus reconstituted the community of Brethren knights, he suddenly found himself at once face to face with the breath of the late Commander; and so by this same mode of information, on which his authority rested, he seemed to have introduced, with the breath of the Commander, a manner of investigation entirely contrary to his own, to which the Bronze Serpent lent the appearance of ritual. That now he suddenly hastened to resort thereto himself and so to render justice to the Commander, his virtual rival, such was indeed the effect of the shock he had just suffered; he fell right into the trap he had wished to avoid, and thus wary from his long experiences beyond the grave, he entered the Chamber of the Bellows as into a place where he would be most safely sheltered from the spiritual solicitations of limitless space.

Consequently, as soon as they saw him enter, the Commander and the other two dignitaries understood that an event had taken place: for as the Grand Master whirled in an ever tighter coil, his robe hugging his obliterated contours, they discerned at its apex the twofold gleam of his gaze. Then, responding with renewed stability, their own whirlings took a similar turn: each one, having bowed before him, entered the upper stall along the left wall, whence they observed the actions of the Bronze Serpent in the fireplace at the rear.

After having intoned the *Veni Creator Spiritus* and recited psalms of penance, the Commander invited the Grand Master to bless the instruments and the lay Brethren: the latter, having beat their breasts three times, then activated the double bellows. At once the enormous leather valves swelled to bursting with a howling roar. It was the first moment of the throng. The lay Brother on the right side ceased his efforts and crossed his arms. The lay Brother on the left side began his own, and released the first breath to come through the tube.

In the hearth, the embers burst violently into flames beneath the Bronze Serpent; once it is white hot, the lay Brother on the left side, gripping its tail between his tongs, fits it to the bellows' tube; slowly the metallic reptile begins to writhe; it quivers and ripples in successive rapid coils, as a still unarticulated moan runs through its entire length; it attempts to gather itself into a triple and then a double coil and at last raises its hollow, incandescent head; from its half-closed jaws escapes a prolonged whistling:

"I'm thirsty! . . ." interprets the Commander.

From a bowl on the end of a stick it is poured a draught of vinegar. Rising from between its fangs and raging, the vapor hesitates to take shape; but this is but a prelude. At the sight of this simulacrum, the Grand Master cannot help but shrug his shoulders. Still, prompted by the Commander, he asks the ritual question:

"Is it you? Whoever you may be, speak: by your word, is it really you?"

Suddenly bending into a single enormous coil as if about to strike, the Serpent opens its maw, jaws distended in a hideous belch, and vomits a sphere of fire.

"I am come!" cries a virginal voice.

So impetuously did she utter these words from the depths of the dazzling sphere that she drove the Brethren Breaths whirling to the floor at the other end

48

of the chamber; yet it was not fright but rather pure decorum that kept them prostrate; for too sweet was the fervor emanating from this sphere, and since they could no longer bear to breathe the penetrating odor that spread about the room, as soon as they saw the breath of the Grand Master prowling towards the hearthstone—and as the Commander, incensed by what had become of his own secret mode of information, had signalled to them to leave the premises—all five of them hastily glided out of the room, the three dignitaries already reeling from intoxication, the two lay Brethren no longer able to contain their hilarity.

"Why did you choose to come in this manner?"

"Outside I spoke to you inside yourself, but you preferred to seek certitude here, in these vile instruments!"

"Now that you are here, I shall destroy them, O heavenly fire that nothing could ever extinguish, even if such were your desire! Among so many expired breaths, when one seems to insinuate its avowals into my own, am I not many a time surprised to find myself in the wrong? With so little trust in my feeble resources, often have I been reduced to consulting this white-hot metal witness! Terrible thoughts have hunted me down like a maddened beast in its cave, to the depths of this smithy of judgment. Were they yours, O Theresa?"

"I call to witness this same Bronze Serpent, so complaisant to your wise imposture: such is the wish of this symbol of that which devours its own tail! For, vomiting all that refuses ever to come back once and for all, so did it vomit me as if I had just expired yet again, since you dread the murmurs of the dead less than the warnings of spirits. That which you could not bear to hear outside your limits you must now hear again, and worse, inside your own enceinte. Listen: two beings are approaching unawares, breathing inside their own bodies at this very moment. By none of your crude and simple-minded ways could you ever recognize their true souls. I know their destinies, their origins, which injunctions on this side of their births they both obey! He, a soul I had torn away from a thousand deviations. . . ."

"What are you going to tell me?" the breath of the Grand Master began to shudder, for according to the law that rules souls separated from their bodies, any personal confession, received outside his charge, inevitably altered his will to the extent that he followed what another breath was confiding to him.

"Let us climb again the slopes of a distant sorrow, without fear: I shall abuse neither your circumstance nor your condition, and far from diverting your attention from your holy ministry, I shall steady you in it. No one has ever known what I am about to unveil to you, a sad story that begins with a mutual lie; grave are its consequences beyond our lives. A young theologian, very able in affairs of this world, once stood behind me with such zeal and devotion at the time of my first foundations and assisted us with such self-denial when our persecutors were bent on destroying the reformation of our Order, that I did not hesitate a moment to choose him as confessor for my first communities. So great was my trust that, on the eve of my departure from one of these holy establishments, it was to him that I wished to confess myself; he stopped me, proclaiming himself unworthy to hear me out: all that he had done for the Carmelites theretofore had been entirely for the sake of the only deity he worshipped: myself! Never had he had any

faith or religion save that! If there really was a provi-
dence, it was only at my side that he would wait for
it to give some sign of his unlikely salvation, and
thenceforth it was up to me either to turn him away
or to keep him, if I did not want to have his perdition
on my conscience . . . . I neither turned him away nor
saw him again. However great was the bliss and
beatitude with which the Lord filled me, however
great the mortifications I inflicted on myself upon my
return in my unworthiness, it seemed that not even the
harshest of these would ever equal the mere thought
of this affliction. Each day I withdrew from him more
severely, until at last I could discern no more than the
dark cloud he had become in his sorrow on the
horizon of my life. For a long time after my death he
compelled me to haunt his desolate nights; the more
I prayed for him the more he invoked the form of my
dust and the more lugubriously took delight in it,
reading and rereading a phrase that I had written one
day in the fallacious sincerity of my heart, to narrate
the petty crimes of my youth: ' . . . I began to wear and
to wish to charm by my appearance, taking great care
of my hands and my hair, using scents and all the
vanities I could obtain. But the more transparent and
light I became, the more substantial my ashen remains
became to his overwhelmed senses. Since his mis-
guided grief had afflicted his powers too much for him
ever to try to practice the ways traced by the Lord in
my thoughts, he flooded his memory with such sorrow as to undermine his reason; but since he gave
his will over to a suffering as obstinate as it was fatal,
this in itself was imputed to righteousness and, when
he expired, my prayers obtained for him a new delay:
I absorbed the suffering of his will but not the sorrow
of his memory: for, as a pure reflection of those words

I had written once long ago—since it was only by that thereafter indelible phrase that he breathed—not only did his breath still seek me in the deceptions of my youth, but these words were never separated from his spiration, and thus he was sent into being a second time. But then, having merged by affinity with a spirit whose vainglorious powers excelled in suggestion, he drove him to forge my double in a state of rapture by means of a detestable simulacrum. Since the sadness implicit in this ruse was again imputed to righteousness, when he expired a second time, covered with earthly glory, a third delay was granted him. Nevertheless, the indelible words still subsisted in his breath; and once he found himself merged anew with a spirit who, alone, would have breathed only piety itself, this merging gave rise to an anxious nature which the pernicious resonance of these words caused to founder in remorse and doubt. Until the day when the Thrones and Dominions deemed that a new creature was destined for him below. God in His prescience knew that this new delay, once he had granted it to my prayers once more, could not ever be the last, so I believed: does He not indeed want the blessed souls continuously to intercede on behalf of the sinners? Could it also be that He would have the same substance remain the same only to fall lower still, because fall He knows it will? Why then did He grant me this delay? Was it to show me that so many returns to existence further aggravate the transgression if it has not been committed once and for all, and changes nothing of the essence of an unexchangeable being? But was this still the same being for whom I had interceded, as it was the same words I had written that depraved him? Could it be my own prayers, like that sentence, which kept him miserable through so many transformations? Or, since God no longer damns or sanctifies any beings whatsoever, might it no longer be sinful to have magnified a transgression from one supposite to the next without any one of them being absolutely guilty of it? Is there henceforth nothing left but effervescences lost in limitless space? If nothing ever happens without God's knowing it and wishing it, it must be that in knowing this, so He wished it as well: He knew in advance that I would not tire of praying to Him, just as he also knew in answering my prayers that at some time the very thing which the conditions of the first existence, the only one that should have remained unexchangeable, did not permit, would be realized in a third existence; and that once the second existence was granted to this expired breath blown back into another, nothing would ever happen again once and for all, if in fact this same breath continued to exist as it breathed those indelible words; and that therefore, in this third life, if indeed it was for the same wretch that I had obtained it by the Mercy of God, nothing would prevent a fourth, a fifth life, and so on one after the other, again and again, from holding up to mockery the Mercy I had begged! And indeed, I wagered against divine prescience, even if it meant winning against myself; for either the memory of those words would fade at last that their true meaning might appear to the new creature destined for this same unhappy soul, provided that the breath so many times expired and redrawn had by then forgotten me—though in this case that soul would no longer be the same; or else the meaning of those indelible words, far from revealing itself, would become entirely obscured in the form of the new creature sent to save him, if indeed that unhappy soul is still enough the same to find me in her—once again!

53

For in fact, all that I had once renounced in myself, recording it in those fatal words, came to constitute the substance of her physiognomy: pure in her beauty but unbelieving, this creature would test the choice of the 'better part' in him; he himself could only atone for his first and only unexchangeable life if he brought this unbeliever once and for all into eternity. Thus they were united. But here a kind of lament was raised up to me—and God must have wanted this too, then, since He knew it in His prescience of all things: far from breaking the spell, this union was consecrated, and the stuff of this sacrament was perversity! . . . His gaze, yes his gaze remained the same, the same that had deceived me! But it was no longer the serene vision that he pretended to seek in my spirit, nor, as he swore, in me! It was my shame . . . and the shame of souls has become his fodder . . . . And there is nothing in the physiognomy of that girl that does not incite him to perpetrate with her what he once thought to have wished in vain to perpetrate with me! All that had been denied him then he now takes out on this creature; he closes off eternity to her, though it had been open so many times to him. Thus is he failing the test. Pure and honest, she does good of her own accord, and this is why she does not believe! and to obey her strange husband in evil is again to her mind a way to do good! And so she truly thinks to do good, just as he truly thinks to do evil! For it has never been but my absent self that he imagines, my shadow he pursues after so many centuries, my spirit he wants to outrage! So great is his despair for not having been able to use me as he now freely abuses her . . . . First he lent her to his friends . . . and now he is forcing her to sell herself! And just as he had once exposed me to the eyes of all, covering my thoughts with a mask

54

fashioned from a sinful pleasure, so too does he make of this unhappy creature my sordid counterpart . . . . Look! Oh, look!"

"No, Theresa, I wish to see nothing!" groaned the Grand Master, choking with terror; curled in upon himself he sighed:

"Who would ever have believed, who would ever have thought to believe that such a brilliant serenity could be still subject to the hyperboles of indulgence! It took the spectacle of these inconstant natures, the perdition of these wills, so flattering to our own security, to awaken your solicitude . . . . Ha!"—he said suddenly.

Silent once more, the sphere of fire had taken on a hue of livid gold: the oval of a face took shape, the eyes closed, the lips parted.

"There she is as I am forbidden to see her!" whispered the Grand Master's breath. May the Rule save me now, O holy Rule, which even here protects us from the stirrings of a fleshly heart . . . ." And regaining possession of himself:

"O Theresa, unworthy as I am, I remain responsible for the tranquility of the higher circles. Just to hear you is to put it all into question! . . . your powerful words upset the order of the ways . . . ."

Then, for having revealed an obliterated recess of her heart to this whirlwind that was questioning her, she in turn saw him as he had once appeared at the heart of the fire in the white robe of a condemned man: the bald head, the face pale and gray, the long nose and thin lips; beneath a shining forehead, his eyes in their sockets expressed only shock and sorrow. Thus the effect of what he had wanted to show her came about then and there.

Theresa slowly lowered her eyes, then raised them

again and looked at him with compassion. Although she knew herself to be all vaporous, a blush colored her cheeks, a very ancient blush as if her blood, once shy in the presence of a man, had broken the ices of oblivion and awakened from its shadowy dryness.

Touched by such sublime ingenuousness, the Grand Master had some difficulty speaking with more severity to this proud soul:

"Is it not at the very least foolhardy to maintain that everything that you have cut off from yourself according to the flights of your spirits could ever have been attributed to the substance of a nature so totally opposite from yours? Was this not preserving the very thing you had abolished forever? That on the other hand a breath, already expired but perverted during the course of its carnal life, should find itself once again reunited with other souls successively created; that this breath should have come to distress them so grievously, unbeknownst to one another, that not a single one was ever sure of having lived his own life once and for all in his own flesh or of otherwise knowing his own immortality without its having been purified in subsequent lives—and that these latter, nevertheless, should have lent themselves to an even greater corruption: I can admit all this as the necessary consequence of the inconstancy of created natures, but—although I do not at all wish to imagine that such an inconstancy could be so invincible as to supplant grace positively in substance—whether or not it pleases God to close the number of the elect, and far be it from the rest of us, here, ever to calculate this mysterious number, as it is your right, O learned Theresa—could He in His almightiness simply limit such a decree of His wisdom? What am I saying? Would I constrain him by an expedient so unworthy of His glory, that He might draw the matter of a new creature from the *peccavi* of his blessed creatures? . . . And although in you I see the radiant mirror of the highest spheres of blessedness, still you sustain this monster at the bottom of the cesspool to the point of granting him, in the form of an inconceivable recreation of yourself, that which for an eternity had returned to oblivion?"

"Ha! What concern is it of yours, Grand Master, if I return there utterly?" thundered the sphere of fire in which the holy visage vanished forthwith. "May God obliterate me! He shall not obliterate me until He surrenders himself! May He surrender! May He Himself fill the void I shall leave! And now as I lose myself in breaths approaching dissolution, you shall see: when their bodies have exhaled them, even before you interrogate them, such a dissonance of voices shall be raised from the depths of their expiration that you shall never be able to differentiate each and its own. Too many debts have they contracted for the creditor-breaths of depravity not to assail them here: destined for the worst of whirlings, their souls shall be dislocated! This is why I, who alone can see them, can do nothing for them here if I show myself as God knows me: these souls could not see me without blaspheming! I must meet blasphemy face to face; I must myself assume its form! Thus shall I turn them away from the impure breaths that I absorb! O Master, in your hands I lay my serenity."

"Haven't you said enough! Do you wish to make me an unjust judge!" cried the Grand Master, breathing himself out on the floor before the Bronze Serpent's smoking maw. But in vain did he invoke the features of the sweet visage in the incandescent sphere:

"You lived a virgin, and a virgin shall you return!"

he roared. "Your place is not here amongst my Brethren! If I keep you, the curse of God shall fall upon the Holy Order!"

"You dare remind me of my carnal state!" uttered the sphere, creating such high flames in the hearth that the metallic device began to melt. "Know that thousands of bodies, male or female, would never suffice to match my powers!"

Heavy smoke spiralled up and slowly rose through the chimney. There was a moment of silence, a rumbling of muffled thunder far away, then silence again; then a sudden crackling against the windows and at last, bouncing against the stone of the fireplace and the ashes, hailstones by the dozen and then by the hundreds piled high.

Suddenly the sounding of a horn burst into the night. Voices called out and shouted commands. The sound of a cavalcade echoed in the courtyards, followed by the whinnying of chargers.

Then someone knocked on the door of the chamber. Since no voice responded, the Seneschal and two squires rushed inside. They found the Grand Master lying on the flagstones, face to the floor; beside him was the gaping and now cold maw of the Bronze Serpent. The Seneschal gently touched him on the shoulder. The Grand Master raised his head.

"Sir Jacques, the King has just arrived and asks you for asylum for a retreat of several days. The rabble is snarling again."

"Why must he always speak of the rabble for these mock retreats!" asked Sir Jacques, quickly standing. "Very well! reserve him the right wing and the north tower. Bring a coffer of crowns to his room at once. How much is in the one from Cyprus?"

"Two thousand pounds!" whispered the Seneschal.

58

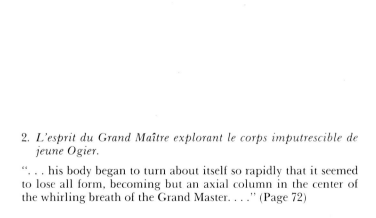

2. *L'esprit du Grand Maître explorant le corps imputrescible de jeune Ogier.*

". . . his body began to turn about itself so rapidly that it seemed to lose all form, becoming but an axial column in the center of the whirling breath of the Grand Master. . . ." (Page 72)

"Add to it the one that came to us from London. Otherwise we'll be seeing him prowling about here till All Saints Day! We welcome him with courtesy and charity: but may this courtesy and charity remain as silent and distant as possible. Prepare everything according to the rites of the first degree. Do not include the signs that announce the second! Replace the emblems with figures that engage the imagination. If he asks you questions on this subject, beat your breasts for every answer. The more contrite we are, the more he will nod his head in understanding. He thinks he's keeping his pledges. That's enough for him."

As soon as he had dismissed them, the Grand Master headed towards the so-called Tower of Meditation. In another age an oratory had been walled up there, by his command, on the eve of the trial. An eternity had passed since he could remember having inspected the place. Anyone in the state of an expired breath—the lowest of rogues as well as the King or the Pope—could have slipped inside. That none had ever entered, except perhaps for the Brethren, was a certainty in that no perceptible reaction from the ones or the others had ever betrayed their having seen the remains inside the oratory. No doubt this precaution was necessary each time the King announced a visit. Sometimes he was simply there, without having given notice of his presence. Since he had been admitted as a member of the Brotherhood, he was allowed, dressed in the robe of a Templar, to lose himself in the crowd of Brethren, on the pretext of humility. He had maintained this custom and practiced it with even more astuteness in the state of an expired breath.

III

The Grand Master concentrated all the will remaining in his breath on that remote event. Letting himself drift with the air currents that whistled through the spiral staircase, he found again, in the same place as long before, the decision he had made and communicated to the Commander to wall up the door. The scene that he himself had not witnessed presented itself anew, just as the Commander had later described it to him, and the same repulsion, mingled with curiosity, overcame him

In the past, in avidly seeking out the horror, his curiosity had not been able to overcome his aversion, whereas now it was free of the dead emotion of disgust. But suddenly the horror came over him like a liquid through the stone, and without effort he found himself inside the oratory.

Seven jumbled masses of coats of mail, ashen forms and long, hairlike filaments intertwined with spider webs; downy vegetation and colorless moulds completely covered the flagstones. A silvery sheen of teeming vermine flickered alternately with the emerald reflections of swarms of flies in flight.

In exploring the space, however, he thought that his own heart, consumed for centuries, had reconstituted itself in the center of his will and was now beginning to beat again.

Beneath the high, arched-vault, suspended in the void, the naked body of a splendid youth slowly turned about itself: the eyes closed, the hanging head bristling with abundant black hair spread out in thick curls over the frail shoulders, a shred of rope around his neck.

In its rotation, every facet of his livid epidermis came into view: the chest, belly, smooth flanks, firm buttocks and perfect contour of his legs; without the short, wide phallus and plump testicles, one would have taken him for a girl, nervous hands still bound behind his back.

Neither the hanging of a child nor the circumstances of the execution that he himself had ordered accounted for the movement that led the old Templar to approach the object of his vision: that youthful body concealed a lie. It seemed of another consistency than the walls or the stone of this ancient fortress that hid him here within its vaporous garrison.

The Grand Master asked himself how it was that he could discern the palpable form of this strangled youth. Until then, he had only glimpsed whirlwinds of expired breaths; and in as much as his own inquisitorial breath was able, by disengaging them from their fortuitous envelopments by other breaths, he managed to assign them more or less probable physiognomies, detached from their long-vanished pretexts, only thanks to his own understanding. How much effort had he wasted on the vain concern that such attributions should not be lost in arbitrary insufflations!

For he was but sleepless volition to which befell only all that he had once had the strength to prohibit in his own mortified body. Now that nothing beyond his ashes confined his henceforth inexpirable breath any longer, his will, pursuing a flight in which he only whirled around himself, could no longer disentangle itself from his own whirlings until he encountered another will no less bewildered than he. This was why he had accepted to return to his charge of Grand Master and to ensure the serenity of the higher circle, whose circumference he knew from his own refusal ever to enter into that region where there is no longer any circle whatsoever, where peace itself wordlessly absorbs all volition: he knew it and this was all he knew. But he was waiting for the restitution of his body in the century to come, and on this pretext he prolonged his wanderings among the air currents of the Commandery of the Temple, where long ago he had been betrayed by his rival, the Commander, won over to the cause of the King. In the absence of his body, this proud ruin constituted his place and his vessel as though ringed by a shadow of resentment which, beyond the forgiving of offenses, provided him with a sense of direction and like an axis inside the whirling he had become, with all the temporary population contained therein and the uncertain ministry of other whirling wills over which he exercised jurisdiction—he attributed the fact that it appeared groundless to him to Philip and the Gallican Sorbonne—allowed him to delay an inconceivable peace: for he continued to believe in the virtue of names, with all that this implied (the principle of contradiction, identity, responsibility, etc.) and in the reason of the whirling column of air through which he moved about by risings and fallings or discrete moves within his own space—and hence also in the dignity of the breath that breathed itself out in designations as much to establish itself as to lay other foundations. In this way he attempted fallaciously to distinguish between his own breath and others, and to postpone as long as possible the merging with the unique Breath, but this struggle proved unequal not only because a violent aspiration promises in advance to each breath a blissful merging with the unique Breath, but also because all the breaths come to agglomerate themselves in one irresistible mass as they are released from their disaggregated bodies: More or less sinful inside the bodies that they agitate below and propel towards order or disorder, they rose to the Commandery with more or less intensity, without it being reasonably possible to sort them out along the way or to ascribe these greater or lesser degrees of intensity to breaths of malice, of probity, of generosity or of avarice, qualities born of the contractions or dilations of bodily organs while the breath was impatiently making use of them, deluding itself as to their mutual origin, whether or not it found itself there confined. If no relation could any longer be established between the forsaken body and the breath whose whirling intensity was no different from that of any other breath—and the violence, moderation or weakness of each of these intensities did not fail to emanate equally from diametrically opposed bodily comportments—how not to risk wronging the fervor of a pious soul whose whirling motion perfectly resembled that of a soul still hot from crime? How not to give offense to pure humility when such a breath, in scraping the ground, could be compared to the grovelling movements of history's greatest traitors? when the apparent, soaring immobility of some breath, lately held in contemplation by the highest spheres, had nothing here to distinguish it from a stagnant, foul nappe, equally phosphorescent, and apparently emitting a flaccid scent of lust? Apparently, alas! And it must have been separated from its body more than once, and must have taken it back more than once—this breath that had received repeated separations like the gift of distinguishing spirits!

Could he even discern the age-long orientation of breaths unenveloped like his own? Languor, contraction, gasping, death-rattling, expansion—all observable once he had cloistered them in staircases, turrets or cells—did these denote the contents of intentions? They were all vestiges, certainly, but of what vanished acts? That which a breath had produced in a woman's body during its earthly sojourn, thereafter vibrating more or less according to the instrumentation of her organs, would break away in a muted resonance of anxiety, saturation or despair—how was this different from the tonality of a young hero fallen on the battlefield? Carried off in its infinite spiral, this expiration would then encounter others: all obstinate, some from regret, some from a satiety to be renewed, some from an obsession, others from a distressing bitterness, all far from the source of this obstinacy now without object, unaware of their reason, reduced to their emotions on the wind, pure exhalations; and each of these breaths would lose itself in the effluvia of another, in accordance with the immediate assimilation with which each was endowed, the most voluptuary as well as the most chaste, the most criminal as well as the most innocent; but by now there was no longer anything criminal or innocent in these unfetterings where the breath of a child might pass into that of an old trooper or a courtesan; the transposed laws of attraction and repulsion brought them into temporary combinations, and while the cluster thus formed of diverse dispositions would thereby enrich itself to the point of experiencing shudders of sensual pleasure and disgust, in this same cluster an overwhelming need to reproduce these sensations would arise and simulate an ephemeral unity; a fallacious exchange of tenderness and insults would then traverse the interlocked spirals of these aimless volitions; yet if chance decreed that a particular resonance should be found again to be such as it had been at the final moment of the separation of one of these breaths from its organs, either the breath, in a burst of memory, would impose it upon the other spirals, or their cluster would shatter: nothing any longer prevented them from carrying on their arbitrary intertwinings, and once again their movement dispersed them far from one another, separated by an eternity.

Now, the Grand Master received as many breaths as his fortress could hold: he knew that if he raised the drawbridge they would enter through the chimneys, and that even if he detained them by force, nothing would prevent them from fleeing as they had come; sometimes he would sit long at his window contemplating the foliage of the vast forests that bent and twisted as if to signal him, bustling in the furious gusts of the whirlwinds, his future guests, who, venturing near his defense walls, were unconcerned whether they entered or not; but he knew himself to be guilty of leaving them outside in their ignorance: inside, calm had just returned; nevertheless, the lack of space was but a pretext; when he spoke of enlarging the fortress, the Visitor to the Order smiled: not only were there other Commanderies, but this one extended as far as the eye could see, here crossing the hills, there rising again above the valley; one had only to climb up one or the other to see it. But this question of place was in fact the same in the attitude that one breath assumed in regard to other breaths: if the breath must reinhabit a body, its own, after its expiration has cast it off, interior as it was, once it is outside itself in a state more inside itself than it had ever been, it is never again in place, for as a breath it has the ability to be spread anywhere as if it had always been so. Called upon to reinhabit its body as if to reinhabit itself, indeed all of itself in one of the myriad dwellings of the house of the Father, it could never find the way there by its own movement unless in the interim it had renounced breathing itself everywhere, no matter how much it might be driven to do so by an apparent enticement to lose itself in its own intimacy turned limitlessly inside out. Thus, as a breath, it needs to accustom itself to an enclosed space, a home, so that from being a diffused intensity it may return to the state of intention, and both sedentary and whirling, it may pass from a roar to a whisper.

But if they were to be brought to the invention of such a home and made to linger in the fortress, the breaths had to recognize it not as their own place, but as their own absence in this place; not at ease as they had been outside when moving inside themselves, here they would be brought to fulfill their intentions. And nothing seemed more appropriate to this effect than the rule and the emblems of the Holy Order; no place was more propitious than this ancient citadel to situating the breaths in the unlikely interval that separated them, as if eternally, from the dust that had expired them.

A breath that is only transparent space, to the point of considering everything that happens to it as being inside itself, only creates, in its aimless intention, imagined exteriors, no less than does this intention itself. When it meets another breath, they imagine each other mutually; but each one does so according to a variable intensity of intention.

In order to ensure that his breath was truly that of the Grand Master, he had ruminated over the indifference of his vacuity, struggling to imagine his improbable ministry through intervals of expiration and inhalation within the indifferentiated vacuity of his own name; in so doing he was able to differentiate himself from the indifference he shared with the other breaths by means of an intention he imagined as much inside himself as pertaining to his Brethren, provided that they in turn imagined their own indifference to be the object of his entreaties. Only the sounding of the Angel's trumpet on the final day, once again reuniting the breaths with their bodies and awakening the latter by means of the former, would put an end to the fragility of the imagined Holy Order.

Having been too long accustomed to the analogousness of being, on which he had grossly relied during his lifetime in the material world, he was all the more troubled by it in his floating state before he decided to improvise a quite rudimentary code which, better suited to the unpleasant surprises of these regions, might keep him from falling back into exegetical pitfalls feasible in the valley of tears but inopportune here. This modification of his judgment, stemming at first from the desire not to be deceived or sidetracked before he could hope to grasp what was occurring both around him and inside him, he achieved slowly and through a kind of sympathetic simulation, letting himself drift, not without distaste, into the comportments of breaths expired before his own: and if indeed these comportments truly corresponded to intentions, again it was necessary not to allow himself to be contaminated in understanding them.

Assuming the guise of many different shapes, each breath, he thought, distinguished itself by its own way of agitating the void as though familiarizing itself with futility, sometimes seeking as well to accommodate itself with another vaster, emptier breath—here, emptiness inspired no fear whatsoever! He would have had to relinquish all notions of a corporeal or terrestrial past, together with the axiom that the soul is the form of the body, in order to discern the contents of an intention, whatever it might be, here in the absence of a space where breaths could freely expand, where nothing any longer distinguished one soul from the next: hence the infinite and apparently gratuitous diversity of the shapes that could divert any judgment of value: spheres, disks, angles, cones, flat surfaces stretching to infinity, straight, undulating or zigzagging lines, simple points: so did the Grand Master experience them himself when he succeeded in isolating a breath from the others in the void of his own void: as disconcerting as was his apprehension in seeing the void alternately coiling and whirling, still sometimes the sight of it puckering into a fixed center seemed to make the conjecture of an outcome possible; nothing, however, was closer to the worst kind of malice than when the void became pure and serene once more, and a breath became a simple, immobile point. Arbitrary perhaps, but malicious in what sense and in relation to what?

The sudden vision of the young body suspended in the void in the high rotunda gave the Grand Master just as much cause for reflection.

"It is indeed a body," he said to himself, "but although lifeless, it is not a corpse." While far from plausible, this distinction corresponded to the general situation of the Temple. Here one could see everything that was analogous to that which one was oneself: breath, whirlwind—but not that which one had ceased to be: corpses or living, palpable bodies. This one was neither alive nor tainted by corruption. The face of the strangled youth bore none of the hideous alterations that usually result from this manner of torture.

"It is a body in dormition: thus its presence here is a fraud."

Having reasoned thus, the Grand Master found himself strangely drawn to the hypothesis that the supreme Breath had himself assumed the form of this body, to preserve himself in its freshness, beyond death.

"He is beautiful as an angel!" he caught himself saying. "But if it is the supreme Breath that sustains him, may I even approach him? I, deprived of my own body, am but a breath without being pure spirit— indeed I see him not with the spirit's eyes but with the eyes of an absent and abolished vision: for there is a difference between perceiving an object about which one thinks, an object tangible enough for the thought to amuse itself with it or to come back to it, and thinking to the point of perceiving impalpable sights, which are all that is granted to us here: any doleful or wailing breath would disturb me less than this unveiled body, which looks to be even lighter than the most vaporous among us! Or might this vision merely be the product of my vaticinating breath? Could it be my pious emptiness that offers itself this victim, or is this sacrificed plenitude sustaining this enceinte?"

Thus emboldened by these tiresome quibbles, he rushed forth, motivated less by the concern to destroy all suspicious traces in the tower before the arrival of the King than by the sudden desire to test the authority of his breath on this false corpse. Hence with all the violence that the suspicion of a transcendent strategem inspired in his breath, he whirled about the suspended body.

Frolicking in the boy's curls, he whispered three times into his ear:

"If you are sent by God, give me a sign and help me in my distress!"

But the bent head did not raise itself, nor did the vertical position of the suspended body shift.

"Whoever you be," continued the Grand Master, "you who inhabit this tortured body, answer me: is it your own? By the Holy Cross, listen! Cease your movement—if you can! . . . But if you be some expired breath come into this body to withdraw from the rest of our expired breaths, then leave this body to rest in peace, breathe yourself out and explain yourself without delay! If you yourself be he who was tortured, do not hesitate to tell me: what do you see, what do you feel? Is it from suffering or from happiness that you remain thus raised in space? Why do you keep your hands bound? Why this rope around your neck? What keeps you in this place? Speak, I beseech you, do not add to my perplexity."

But as deaf to questions as to entreaties, the adolescent continued to turn slowly about himself in the void: an odd smile froze his lightly parted lips; no breath issued therefrom, no air did his dilated nostrils inhale. So, hoping himself to probe the secret workings of this presence that feigned future glory, the Grand Master tried to breathe himself into the body through its mouth; but as impetuous as he tried to be, far from penetrating this orifice, he was dispersed into a mist around the boy's lips. Long eyebrows shadowed the closed eyelids of this visage absorbed in endless bliss. The body remained inexplorable.

How would the breath of the Grand Master react once it had seized like an absence of breath this youthful perfection in its palpable form? No longer was he up against an externality compliant to his internal imaginings; he was as though inside himself, up against a closed interior; and inside himself, he remained outside; could he, an intelligible void agitated by entreaties, subsume this opacity, which was calm to the point of indifference?

He wanted to regain his breath, the more vehemently to insufflate it into this deaf and dumb perfection.

But when he tried to whirl himself into a larger spiral to assail it once again, he succeeded only in moving away from it: no other movement was permitted him than that of following the rotation of the suspended body.

As though the youth were turning away from all further injunctions, his body began to turn about itself so rapidly that it seemed to lose all form, becoming but an axial column in the center of the whirling breath of the Grand Master. Carried away by the delirious speed, the latter flared out like the orbs of a spinning top; but when the rotation of the suspended body slowed down to its original speed, the Grand Master's whirling divided into three spirals: his perception, his will and his consciousness. The spiral of perception no longer distinguished itself from the spinning motion of the youth, yet it never managed to take in all at once every facet of the body; inside the second spiral—was it rising or falling?—his will was turning to indifference; inside the third, imperceptibly moving spiral, his consciousness exhausted itself in being reflected in the other two. Searching for intention in self-oblivion, his consciousness could no longer distinguish in its purpose the vain pretext of a true motive. Just as his perception had merged with the vacuity filled with the object perceived, so the pretext had become confused with the motive; for although he had entered the cursed chapel to hide all trace of crime from the King, this was not the concern that made him think to inspect the sanctuary. Yet although the questions raised by this phenomenon concerned, to all appearances, the motive, this motive remained masked by the purpose of concealing a crime—not in the indifferent will, but in the consciousness over which this indifference had unfolded as completely as had the perception of that body: thus the manner in which it questioned itself became but a rumination on the indifferent vacuity that his will had once more become, whether in these three spirals his consciousness considered itself as so many differing relationships newly born of his indifference, or whether it had merely lost its way in conjectures and alternatives: for if God kept this breathless body incorruptible, was it to exhort the bodiless breaths to overcome their indifferent freedom or was it, on the contrary, to test their discernment, as if to say: Consider then if this be indeed a hollow form that your emptiness might fill?

So close to touching upon the true motive, his consciousness no longer had the power to answer such specious questions after his perception had already answered them. For the perception of the unimaginable object had abolished with this interval, which he had created for himself to gather himself together when he imagined everything to be within himself: no longer was there time between one thing and the next; his perception had merged at once with all aspects of this body. Therefore, what he perceived in his vacuity, without being able not to wish it, could only by conjecture reach his stupefied consciousness, which all the more weakly rejected what it perceived as it imagined itself in vain among these three spirals, of which it was, for this reason, the least certain. For if his consciousness could have been reflected in all three by one sole spiration, it would only have reestablished the vain pretext of hiding a crime which masked the real motive. Just as it is written: *"In your weakness I am strong"* it was thanks to his stupefaction that the real motive became clear, thus again thanks to his indifferent will that wished that everything he perceived should be perceived as if he had already wished it: hence in perceiving a detail on this body, he could not help but wish this detail as well.

What was it then that caused this detail, which he also could not help but wish, to rouse him from indifference? It was not so much the vain pretext of hiding a crime, nor still the true motive, although the one, so to speak, supposed the other.

It was wrath, suddenly overwhelming his perception, which through a unique spiration reestablished the Grand Master in his intention—not consciousness, which was engulfed in disconcerting syllogisms. And although here wrath had the merit of awakening consciousness to synderesis, still the reason for this escaped him: barely formed like the shadow of a

74

scruple, intention did not even have the time to know its object: it was this object itself, it was this perceived detail.

For in fact, vexed that the noble orifices—the mouth, ears, and nostrils, those symbols of utterance, consent and censure—were forbidden to him, he angrily whirled lower, around the boy's loins: below the wrists tied behind the back, grazing the bloody hands with palms upturned over the buttocks, he hesitated for a long time before the orifice of ignominy.

If access to the anus was also forbidden to his insufflation, he had to acknowledge, if not the evidence, at least the hypothesis that it was the Heavens that sustained this adolescent body in the void, both upright and inaccessible. Here, in this hypothesis that his consciousness posited once again as a reason for his lingering, synderesis was born: then, like a lightning bolt, intention sprang forth in wrath.

Sealing the anus, there shone the diamond of a ring, stamped with the crest of the Holy Order.

None but the vile Malvoisie could have perpetrated this double profanation.

Was it to disavow the defamatory accusation levelled against his Brethren? Was it to avenge himself of the failure of his authority over this body in dormition?

So great was the Grand Master's indignation that he concentrated all the intensity of his breath on the precious stone: who would have believed it? Relinquishing its shining guardian, the gaping, sinister portal beckoned.

Malvoisie had possessed the living body of this youth. Where had the breath of the scoundrel gone? And where that of his victim? He had suffered Malvoisie and yet his exalted martyr's body spurned the breath of the Grand Master! Was he still obeying the breath of the hangman? Was he inside this levitating body or not? A glorified, empty form?

In the diamond nevertheless gleamed the pretext of concealing all traces of crime from the King. But if at this moment the breath of Philip had in turn slipped into the cursed oratory, it would have found the Grand Master in an attitude of confession. Once the ring had fallen, the diamond irradiated the true motive.

Synderesis served as a ladder to his consciousness, which it climbed then discarded as soon as it had emerged from the indifference of the will. The Grand Master had taken back his breath: the gaping orifice was only ignominious in its expectation of his own ignominy. An eternity had just passed. An eternity would pass again: it was necessary that it not be indifferent.

The Grand Master, no less than Theresa—each during his lifetime, though centuries apart, each according to a discipline proper to his condition: Theresa through a life of contemplation, the Grand Master through an austerity both military and monastic—had striven to recognize the maximum burden of sin in his bodily gestures as well as in the stirrings of his flesh, in anticipation of the passage into the totally indifferentiated freedom in which expired breaths exist, that test of absolute arbitrariness in which the God of bodies Himself appears for a moment to sink down with us, forever destroying all our designations. The worst and the highest degree of this test once again required, like a petition for reprieve, an appeal to abominations which no longer betrayed anything indicating that they had ever taken place. Even when guilt had remained virtual in corporeal life, when an assiduous mortification had quelled even the slightest sinful inclinations, it was all the more necessary for guilt to realize itself in the expired breath and for this breath to sin because of indifference, for fear that this indifference, in the bosom of a peace that defied words, should result in a void of all retribution.

Now, the saint seemed less concerned than anyone with the resurrection of the body, although she would have liked to see her own body aflame with divine wrath, suffering through eternity, incandescent with what to her eyes was only supreme love; and consenting to the law that expropriated not only all flesh from its breath but all breath from its spiritual qualities, she in turn had known the waywardness of an aimless wanting, an intention without content, dispersed among other breaths—unworthy, no doubt, of ever encountering her—and like them she was a languid, contracted, panting or expanded breath: for supreme love, certainly; but as even here she in no wise pursued her own interest (which, had she ever done so during her lifetime, would have also been of complete indifference to her), nothing prompted her to withdraw from the other breaths, though they were impure, criminal or lustful in origin; borne up into the clusters of these spirals and lending her splendor to ignominy—into God only knows what strange clusters, mingling what was best in her with what was the worst in others—she too formed temporary "cumuli" in the intermediary regions between the fleshly, corruptible worlds and the higher heavens.

Her unconcern with her former meritorious sojourn in her body, her abandon to the state of indifference, her remoteness from beatific vision—so great that he himself had difficulty conceiving it—the Grand Master could only explain by a very simple reasoning that often occurs in military and monastic souls whose condition accustoms them to uttering judgments as peremptory as their slashings of the sword or their signs of the cross: Theresa had had her statue. And what a statue! Could it be that God saw her the way this masterpiece presented her to man's devotion?

The angel slowly raises the arrow with one hand, with the other he draws back the saint's veil and with a tender smile delights in driving her to distraction. What spoils for the victor! Turned completely about, her interior rendered exterior, the banners of the soul unfurled in the frozen swirls of the marble, the ineffable struggle mirrored in her rolling eyes, rising to the surface of her tautened lips, she sighs the bliss of her surrender: here at once is the abyss of her evanescence exalted and her effusions captured in the sole form of the heavenly youth. What she denied as a thorn of lustful pride, the Heavens render unto her on those angelic fingertips: separated from her nature at last, the nascent virility of her spirit attains Theresa's own impossible possession of herself.

The style of this stone simulacrum was not to the Grand Master's taste; nonetheless an unfathomable secret, divulged by this sculpture, provided him the malice necessary to his endeavor.

"Either the higher Circle is a place of shameful spiralling delight, or this anagogical presumption signifies her refusal to resuscitate as woman! So be it! It's for her to stand the test!"

Barely had he insufflated his judgment to this orifice that he still deemed ignoble—forgetting that in an exalted body none of its parts are excluded from its glory—when the heretofore bowed head of the youth righted itself; the eyes opened, the lips puckered, and suddenly, wrists freed from their bonds, his right hand touched his breast while his left hand fell. . . .

— — — —

The Grand Master almost leaped back: and he was whirling, unforeseeably slowly, when his breath was entered seven times by milky seeds: O amazement! his face was streaming—for his sinner's body had come back to him, and as he dried his eyes with his robe, he found himself back on the steps of the staircase.

IV

He was greeted by an ovation the echo of which reverberated from stairway to stairway and off the high vaults of the great refectory.

The unity that had been restored in the Grand Master's breath now gathered outside him and re-grouped the hundreds of intentions imagined to be surrounding his own. In the penumbra of the vast space intersected by cascades of daylight filtering through the stained glass windows above the long tables, hundreds of mouths hummed, hundreds of glances shone: at once joining in a single cry of joy at his entrance to the hall, the Brethren Breaths waited in suspense for his words to make the consistency of each of them reverberate in each; for they were com-memorating the anniversary of his torment as if it were their own, the vain destruction of the Temple and the iniquity of Philip.

Was it necessary or not for them to justify the most obscure of their rites, the spitting on the cross? For did they know, among themselves, what they were denying? Called upon to explain this rite, the Grand Master had confessed to the heresy expressly imputed to the Holy Order:

"For the breath of the Savior was never made flesh, nor did it die, nor resurrect, except in appearance: yet whosoever hears His voice shall shed his own appearance and live forever as breath within the Breath!"

Sir Jacques de Molay had openly retracted such confessions—wrenched from him by his tortures—in his final hour at the stake, before the people. Other Brethren who in the meantime had, like him, retracted their admissions, retracted their retractions, giving breath unto the Breath rather than denying it.

Yet what likelihood was there that he did not believe what he had formerly confessed when in his tortured body, what likelihood that he had disavowed it in a final act of faith? What he refused to believe here he could indeed now see, and still he shut his eyes to the evidence of the only thing that seemed evident: for nothing was less evident to a breath than that a body had ever expired it, a body in which it must resurrect, if only in appearance . . . . His Brethren had spat upon the crucifix to honor the Breath in their breath; now he, with his own breath, spat on this Breath to honor the glory of the tortured Body. Each time perplexity threatened to disunite his spiration, the memory of his final retraction reestablished his unity: and this position of recantation, bequeathed to history, this defiance of the fallacious evidence of a heretical posthumous interval between life in the world and orthodox eternity, formed the basis on which his very memory had here instituted the commemorative celebration of his torment.

He would find his memory back in the high hall of

the refectory. There it sat amidst his thousands of Brethren, table companions at this solemn ceremony; it was only waiting for his breath to return. And once it repossessed it, it sought to spread itself among them once more, pretending to accompany them to the very limits of their wanderings. Thus in these words did it fondly hope to cast doubt in their minds on the evidence of bodiless freedom:

"Dearly beloved Brethren! On this memorable day in which the cycle here completed brings us together yet again before continuing on its course—and may it be the last to separate us!—I give thanks to God for your loyalty! Though you are now released from all oaths, and no constraints could ever more bind your breaths, and your consciousness has spread to the limitless spaces where a thousand combinations call out to you, to which being itself seems to grant the benefit of the doubt, still you have chosen the servitude of your old brotherhood! As strong as may be your inclination to whirl as you wish, yet something draws you to this table: here we find again the gestures of eating and drinking; O blessed custom which in each of us has triumphed over appearances! Our bodies, slowly reduced to ashes, threaten to clothe us again, in the twinkling of an eye . . . . It is out of deference to human society that we feast!

"This is why, beloved Brethren, before we sit ourselves down and speak openly, we shall together make this act of penance:

"Holy earth that we have renounced defending, is it not a mockery that ever since we abandoned you, our brotherhood, our riches, our prestige and our authority have not ceased to grow? But what did we abandon? The empty Sepulchre that bears witness to our survival? But what have we survived? Have we not always been here? . . . Who then revealed this to us, if not he who was buried therein? Who thus pretended to escape from there on the third day, when there was no first day? A breath! But could a breath ever say: This is my body, this is my blood? Unless it were perhaps to mislead another breath that was accusing us? But of what could one breath accuse another? Of the poor use to which we put the bodies created for us? Would a breath ever be so perverse as to put another breath in straits and then reproach him for being ill at ease? Of what then were we guilty down there if not of having been so ashamed to be breaths that we concealed ourselves in bodies? But what is a body to a breath if not its dissimulation? Unless we are now guilty of acting like breaths here, of what indeed were we guilty down there if not of having believed we could not breathe until the day we saw the light of day, and of believing that this breath could expire on a cross! But did he not also say: 'Destroy this temple and I shall rebuild it in three days'? Is this not our motto, the cornerstone against which our detractors waste their energies because it defies the laws of gravity? . . . O my Brethren! Take care not to question yourselves thus, though here you may do so at leisure, in good conscience! Was that not how you were subjected to torture? Did they not produce as proof the very things they made you say? Did your cries under torture renounce the breathless body or . . . the dissimulated breath? . . . Beware, my Brethren; into what kind of truth have you fallen?"— — — —

V

—— —— —— ——

The door appeared walled up again. But leaning against the stone, dressed in the black and white costume of the pages of the Temple, was the same youth—with the gaze and the smile of Theresa.

"What were you doing here?" asked the Grand Master. The question came out of his mouth as if these mistrustful words, provoked by a banal encounter suspended centuries before, in this same place, anticipated a surprise reaction that could not be situated outside of time. *What were you doing here?* The demand of a superior to his subordinate, uttered brusquely, sternly, suddenly admitted this past banality: the living presence of his page surprised him only because he judged it indiscreet and out of place here. What had just taken place in this condemned chapel was perhaps not without witnesses. That the door was walled up again did not reassure him. Everything that happened in this fortress was perfectly transparent, despite the thick walls and the respectful, taciturn bearing of all its occupants. No one needed to mention what everybody saw. On the contrary, in seeing everything, one tended to speak as little as possible. In the past, honesty and charity demanded that one not seek to know what went on even in the cell of the next Brother. Now not one of them could help but see it. If, formerly, one thus became guilty of an immodesty of sight, hereafter, in seeing that which one did not deliberately seek to know, if one kept silent to the extent of overcoming the need to speak (and the Grand Master saw this at once), one became no less guilty of consenting to an accomplished fact, but an unnatural one: *one granted that the soul had never been united with the body* and that personal speech being useless on the pretext that there no longer was any particular interlocutor to whom to address any particular thing, one professed the existence of a sole intelligence, received by each but immediately operating within all, under cover of this silence. Nothing, in fact, was more heretical or more fallacious than this virtue of silence; nothing more immodest than these vacant glances. The very law that ruled the freedom of indifference of souls separated from the body conferred on their worldless intentions an otherwise deadly efficacity: as soon as one pointed out anything whatsoever, beginning with the fact of being able to do without the body, one changed oneself in changing each "interlocutor": one changed oneself in the sense that he who expresses himself bodilessly immediately passes into the thing expressed; and at the same time one changed the one whom one was addressing, in the sense that he who receives the expression of a thing that he nevertheless already knows and sees inside himself, experiences in his very understanding the way of seeing of the one addressing it to him. For the one receiving this new expression only receives after the other has already been changed by articulating it to him; and in receiving it, faced with this change in the "interlocutor," he too cannot resist change, for he too must change in order to understand it. And by no means could he simply refuse: for as their bodies no longer imposed any limits on their respective intentions, they mutually invaded each other. In the absolute transparency in which breaths exist in relation to one another, no self-conceit prevails.

The reciprocal altering of the members of his community made it difficult for the Grand Master to oversee the Brethren knights. Thanks to a resentment born of the Royal offense inflicted upon the Holy Order, he had succeeded in maintaining in each of the Brothers not a thirst for revenge and rehabilitation but, on the contrary, a guilt on the same scale as the injustice suffered: to make oneself guilty so as to turn iniquity into justice! It was the only way for the Brethren Breaths not to lose themselves in each other, aided by too facile a pardoning of offenses, in an irresponsible communing in which the wait for the resurrection of the body was gradually abandoned. For this reason it was necessary for everyone to find himself guilty of pride and indiscretion according to the ancient rule, to satisfy the posthumous rule he had established. One never gave voice to any acts whatsoever without doing so in one's own name. And one only recounted these acts as deeds. There was not a single deed that was not asserted as one's own. Of the blameworthy ones, each competed to accuse himself, claiming them as his own; the praiseworthy deeds were only attributed to others. An illusory competition: who here merited blame or praise? The past was no longer of any consequence, and one had to feign the required interest in it in order to find oneself speciously inside others.

Thus, in observance of the newly instituted rule, the young page responded to the injunction: *What were you doing here?* by answering: "It was to be adored, O Grand Master, that I had myself hanged! And hanged, I found myself adorable, adoring myself as I awaited an adorer!"

For a moment the Grand Master was stunned: to all evidence the youth imagined himself the sole instigator of the meditation interrupted in the walled-up chapel. But as meritorious as was this faithfulness to the letter of the Rule, nonetheless the ruse by which the youth, in so doing, called the Grand Master himself into question, distressed him.

"And this, Grand Master, this is the crime of which Ogier de Beauséant, your humble, loyal and ever obedient servant, accuses himself."

Barely had the youth named himself when this declaration had the effect of throwing the Grand Master into the state that had preceded his agony. For according to the same rule, should not the Grand Master have accused himself in turn of villany and murder, however little he might wish to lower himself to beg the pardon of his young victim? But he couldn't even recognize the victim in the one who had just named himself.

And in fact, in instituting the rule of self-denunciation, he had not foreseen that for a soul separated from its body the act of expressing itself in its own name, even if to accuse itself of an infraction, entailed the same alteration as any other expression of breath, just as this true or false assertion of guilt for the sake of another breath changes no less the latter. And so, to hear the youth give himself the name of Ogier de Beauséant, he himself changed in the sense that the "historical condition" implicit in this faraway name took place in him, and that the content proper to this completed condition immediately filled, as any other content would have done, the perpetual vacancy of his breath.

Now had he not just seen the youth hanging from the vault of the walled-up chapel? Once he was carried away from that place, thanks to the invocation of the saint, he was left with only the confused consciousness of an abomination: nothing was left in him of his discovery—unless it was the suspicion of having been watched, and this alone gave him an uneasy sense of something reprehensible. And this uneasiness, now, on the stairhead, against the stone of the cursed door, took the form of the young boy, daintily dressed in plumed cap, surcoat of black velvet, silken breeches. At the sight of this child of less than fourteen years who said insolent things, the Grand Master forgot even the rule, even the past event of his own agony, and for an instant rediscovered the gestures to which he had been accustomed when alive.

"You haven't yet reached manhood and you dare speak to me in tongues! Enter my cell immediately to be disciplined! . . ."

The one who claimed to be Ogier de Beauséant, in spite of his submissive air, looked at him with a hint of knavishness in his velvet eyes as if, mimicking the profound gaze of Theresa, he couldn't hide the amusement he felt at such a sinister prank. Then seized with a frenetic fury, in a sort of surge of impatience such as sometimes and especially comes to those souls called separated, the Grand Master, seizing the young boy by the collar, pulled off his doublet. The shirt swelled with a panting chest: seeing this, Sir Jacques in his rage tore open the cloth: at once two alabaster maiden's breasts sprang forth. The supposed Ogier de Beauséant, head thrown back, eyelids half closed, kept his lips parted. Exasperated, the Grand Master wanted to throttle him and, oh wonder, he throttled him indeed with the whole force of his vigorous arms: clasping the boy's frail neck and stroking his virginal bosom, his own charred body seemed to recompose itself in the unleashing of the power of his wrath. When the boy's plumed cap fell, the ebony curls spread out over the fleshless, waxen fingers of the old Templar. He had no more doubts: she was a spy sent by the Pope, the King, if not by Nogaret.

"Bitch! sorceress! play-actress! Who brought you into our sacred house in this guise?"

"Before God, I swear to you, my Lord, I am none other than Ogier de Beauséant!"And he raised his delicate hand, on which a diamond sparkled.

Sir Jacques drew back, his fingers twitching in his beard, then with a gesture he ordered the page to remove his breeches. The child made as if to resist; once again his deep gaze penetrated the Grand Master. The latter began to tremble in all his limbs as though their illusory substance reflected, like a defilement, the posthumous profanation of the walled-up chapel. Then, unaware that he was merely venting his rage against the indifferent freedom of his true condition, he seized the boy's codpiece and brutally tugged at the laces.

Barely was this dilemma resolved when a frightful bolt of lightning crashed into the cell.

"At last, Heaven's interceding!" he said to himself, and for the first time since the flames of his agony had opened his breath to the clairvoyance of a limitless day, he groped in the shadows.

VI

But what seemed to him to be complete darkness soon turned mauve, then red, then softened to a blond transparency: indeed, he felt himself as though sheltered there, and relieved of a responsibility as crushing as it was absurd, from which he believed himself redeemed, to the sound of fanfare—perhaps that of his resurrection? For reduced to the simplest expression of the promised flight, but with an added lightness befitting the infinite ripples of beatitude, he discerned at first—thanks to his concupiscent perception that restored to measure the disparity between these flattering proportions and his own appetency— like a tender cloth beneath his frail step, the vast palm of a feminine hand, in whose hollow he imagined himself crouching, whose tapered fingers rested on a sloping hip, immense and immensely naked, that he himself circled, hovering about it on diaphanous wings; there, humming with pleasure, uncertain, he floated between the basin of the navel and the soft slopes of the shady valley. Having wet his slender probe in the humid basin and already drunk, he skimmed the shining, curved air; but frightened by the shadow cast there by the enormous withers of a dragon risen from the underbrush and beating its red poll blindly on its own threshhold, he himself took shelter higher up in the space where the albescent mammillae pointed like snowy heights, even and peaceful in the first rays of dawn, and having decided to land on one or the other not without fearful hesitation, he rose up, in order to descend more prudently, and pretended to lose his way near the nightlike, silken mane that fell in curls from the lowered forehead, when two luminous orbs suddenly stared down at him. Again darkness enveloped him; he barely had the time to inhale the warmth of that place of supple walls of skin—a crack resounded, reverberating endlessly inside him . . . .

Exhaled onto the flagstones by the crushed fly, gasping, would his generous breath ever come back to him? Overwhelmed by lust to the infinitesimal size of a sordid subtlety, he swelled to understand what he had just explored. Begun, all sensual, with the expectation of an innocent dawn, this expedition concluded with a fall so staggering in its lucidity that he could hardly call it a mistake: and to his nostalgia for flourishing asylums was mingled the bitter conviction of having been rejected as unworthy.

So, sighting the still unspeakable presence standing before him, he remained with forehead to the ground, so to speak, less out of veneration than to avoid judging what he had recognized: whether this was Ogier or Theresa, he no longer wanted to know; but his prostration notwithstanding, the inconceivable took shape in his clairvoyance; and although he wanted to concentrate on only one aspect of the radiant nakedness—the torso, seen from the back, and the bowed head of the lad contemplating himself— this figure imposed itself with greater power from the front. The face did not even hide behind the delicate fingers, but the ecstatic eyes, Theresa's own, sparkled beneath the broad arches of the youth's brows.

"Is it really you? No, get back!" he said.

"You are ashamed to invoke me as you see me now, I whom you persecute by the rule you laid down! And now it comes back to haunt you, who at all costs want to keep your Brethren believing in their own bodies! Allow the souls separated from them to express themselves to each other, let them freely change themselves as you have already changed me!"

"I changed you?"

"Look and acknowledge what you see!"

"I see your monstrous body without believing in it, just as I do not believe in my own, of which I am deprived."

"Then cling to your ashes, rediscover them anew, that you may be judged by what you have perpetrated in your body, when they sheathe you again: is this indeed your wish?"

"Of course, for the Judge shall bring justice upon my enemies and shall allow me to see his face!"

"Who are these enemies and what face will the Judge show to you?"

"He knows my enemies and his face shall fulfill me! For innocent did they burn me, and through him shall I be vindicated!"

"And you still believe this?"

"My reason, or what is left of it, resists; but I believe I've lived once and for all in my own body."

"But must you not also be judged for what you have perpetrated in the meantime? Look at this hornet."

"And so?"

"Did you not choose to be born in the body of the Grand Master who was burned?"

"Certainly not!"

"Be careful what you say, Grand Master! Did you or did you not choose the shape of this hornet to savor my navel?"

"You mock me!"

"It is you who mock your resurrection, Grand Master! For if you wish to resurrect in your solemn body, who then shall judge you in this hornet's body? Will it be up to you or to the hornet to repent?"

"I too wish to repent!"

"For the second time, I warn you, be careful what you say: of what will you repent? a peccadillo or a capital sin? Was the impurity commensurable with a hornet or must this fragile insect absorb all the concupiscence of the Grand Master in order for him to resurrect chaste? Is it up to the hornet or Sir Jacques de Molay to atone?"

"I take all the blame upon myself!"

"But did you not lend your most secret intention to the hornet? Here you are now, the expired breath of a hornet!"

"I'm still not convinced!"

"Never mind that," said the immense nakedness. "Let us weigh your breath against this hornet."

"What are your weights and measures?" asked the breath that still believed itself to be Jacques de Molay.

"Your own!"

The nakedness raised two pans of a scale in equilibrium and placed the dead insect on one side of the scale. The pan began to sway.

"Now it's your turn to counterbalance, Grand Master: breathe your entire self onto this pan."

Yet although he made a great effort of concentration, the pan remained raised in the air while the hornet weighed heavily on the other, which would not rise.

"Where have you gone to?" asked the nakedness, shaking his long curls. Batting his lashes, his immense eyes rolled from left to right, and while with the tips of his fingers he was hoisting the beam of the scale, he exposed his armpit and slightly raised the nipple of one of his breasts. As he kept his long hand on his hip, his scepter beat the cadence of his skepticism. But already what was left of the Grand Master's breath on the unbalanced pan dwindled further as it contemplated this insolent figure.

"Could it be your continence that made you so light? What enormous crime gives more weight to this insect than to yourself? You aren't going to pretend that the meaningless innocence of an insect outweighs the historical importance of the Grand Master? For the third time, be careful, Sir Jacques de Molay: or else you shall appear before God as you choose, burdened with this sin as well. Relieve yourself of this insect of your concupiscence, or accept to be punished in this guilty hornet!"

"Haven't I committed enough abominations without adding to them the willingness to listen to your absurd dilemmas . . . ."

"Your abominations are but the feeble spasms of your indifference! Profit at least from this hornet's body to discharge yourself of your debt, if there be any consistency at all to your teaching."

"So be it! I shall expiate this moment of aberration for love of Justice, if that be within your power."

95

Would he have enough time to make up his mind? What notion of justice could he still have? Already his breath had passed into the tight corselet of the insect and once again felt so at ease there that he stood up on his legs and, unfolding his wings, he flew straight from the pan of the scale to the rosy mammillae of the immense nakedness. No sooner had he grazed it when a shooting spark set him aflame: wing pinched between the nails of the gigantic pubescent, the more he struggled, the hotter the flame, and the more he grew in size, the more the flame crackled. Then, discerning through the smoke the shine of those sublime pupils and the vast arch of those smiling sweet lips, he barely managed, parched by a desiccating heat, to buzz: "Have mercy! Have mercy, whoever you may be!"

VII

— — — —

Sir Jacques de Molay had returned to his first state. Dressed in the robe of his day of torment, partially consumed and still smoking, he was kneeling at the feet of young Ogier de Beauséant, embracing his knees. The latter, in his page's habit, held out his slender hands to the old Templar; the Grand Master kissed them.

"My Savior and God!" he stammered.

"Why do you call me savior and god?" asked the adolescent, caressing his cheeks with his palms. "I am not a creator who enslaves being to what he creates, what he creates to a single self, and this self to a single body. O, Sir Jacques, the millions of selves that you oppress within yourself are dead and have resurrected millions of times in you, unbeknownst to your single self."

"Is it not myself that you have just rescued from the flames?"

"Your Creator saved you, He who claims you as his own creature, since you speak to me this way. I do not dispute it! For I am not a master who, like Him, reaps what he has not sown!"

"Whoever you may be, don't leave me!"

"Accept my service and I shall be your loyal servant!"

"What greater service could you ever perform for me than to give me back unto myself!"

"To free you from yourself . . . ."

"From myself? But is it not necessary that I be judged in my body?"

"It is not necessary! It is you who would have it so!—instead of the freedom that you will lose when you resurrect as you are now, the knowledge that you will forget anew when you come to know yourself as your Creator knows you, for better or for worse! But how will you know yourself then? Perhaps as something worse than a fly!"

"Then you should be the King of the Flies for suggesting it!"

"Certainly not! For he created flies too, to inspire you to a higher idea of yourselves! But if you were now to keep your freedom, you would know there is no difference between the bliss of a seraph at the foot of his throne and that of a hornet taking delight in the sweat of my navel!"

"And therein lie your services?"

"So you like your high idea of yourself! I shall remain your forever useless servant! Goodbye then!" exclaimed the adolescent with deep reverence. The Grand Master insistently clung to his legs:

"You're leaving me? Stop," he begged him. "By what name may I invoke you?"

"You refuse my services! What does my name matter

to you? In truth I tell you: the millions of brothers and sisters inside you, who have died for your high idea of yourself, know my name well, and are reborn in it; no proper name exists for the hyperbolic breath that is my own, any more than anyone's high idea of himself can resist the vertigo of my great height; my forehead dominates the stars and my feet stir the abysses of the universe."

Although he was overwhelmed by his physiognomy, such a presumptuous declaration by the graceful pubescent did not fail to appear ridiculous to the old Templar, and this flash of reason momentarily erased from his memory all that had just transpired to effect his being there, clinging to the page's knees, drawing them tightly to his breast, slipping his hands between the boy's thighs. The latter, knitting his brows, made a gesture to free himself.

"What is this unspeakable name?"

"You're not preserving your gravity, Grand Master! It's useless to tell you: one cannot remember it as long as one is still coming back to oneself."

"Spell it for me, I beg you, so I will have invoked you but once!"

The adolescent began:

"B-A . . ."

"Ba . . . ?" repeated the Grand Master.

"P-H-O . . ." continued the adolescent.

" . . . pho . . . ?"

"M-E-T . . . ."

" . . . met! . . ."

The youth suddenly pointed his finger at him:

"What is your name?"

"Why . . . Jacques de Molay . . . alas!"

"How do you call your faithful servant?"

Still crouching, Sir Jacques let his arms fall. The

adolescent, now freed from his grasp, stepped back a pace.

"Sir Jacques de Molay, time is running out. I cannot repeat my name to you. Too respectful of the Creator, I loyally comply with the covenant that binds us: memory is his domain, mine the self-oblivion of those reborn in me. And I shall take care not to remind Him that before creating the rest of you, he caused thousands of gods to die within Himself in order to create Himself unique! I can do nothing against the memory He leaves to his creatures."

"Wait!" cried the Grand Master, extending himself his entire length, arms stretched towards the young page who was already turning his back to him. Turning right about, the other replied:

"O Grand Master, speak before you return to the state of a forlorn whirlwind! What more do you wish to learn?" added the adolescent, but what shone in his eyes was all Theresa's compassion.

"Already I no longer know what I must say to you. Help me!" whispered the Grand Master, "Help me, since you do know!"

"Do you then accept me? Decide!"

"Interrogate me, or else ineptitude will strangle me . . ." said the Grand Master, breathless.

Then, nearing his shining virgin face to the sere, ashen countenance of the warrior-monk and grazing it with his long ebony curls, the youth whispered to him:

"Do you not now repent having fled before the dragon of the shady vale?"

"O, I die of shame!"

"Is this not the very thing you could not bring yourself to confess to me?"

"Indeed!"

"But if you are now ashamed of it, is it because you would not hesitate to fight it like the valiant knight you are?"

"Certainly!"

"But would a valiant knight bother to avenge the cowardice of a hornet?"

"It would be beneath him!"

"Could it be that you are instead ashamed of your remorse?"

"O give me the opportunity to confront it again!"

"But," continued the adolescent as he turned away, "what if the knight in his bravery went so far as to fight the dragon with only a hornet's defenses? Would it not be more dignified and right to triumph thus?"

"What do you mean to say?"

"To triumph, he must drink deep from the wells of the mammillae and draw therefrom the power necessary to his sting: then shall he fly to attack the dragon, and if he captures it, the dragon will surrender its liquid treasure!"

"Do you take me for a fool?" cried the Grand Master, suddenly standing, "and will you obey me at last, rascal!"

He had rushed forward, but fell into his own void: his floating state had returned.

"Ah! Where was I? What did I say? Where am I?"

"Outside the burnt body of the Grand Master, as befits his expired breath?"

"Which Grand Master?"

"Be faithful to your oblivion!"

"Baphomet, Baphomet; who are you then in my oblivion?" he asked, whirling around the youth whose visage was now squeezed into a wimple. With one of his beautiful hands the youth lightly parted his Carmelite veil.

"The Prince of Modifications!" she said, batting her long lashes while her fingers toyed with a rosary knotted around the sash of a black robe flowing in long folds to her feet. "In truth I tell you: whosoever nourishes his oblivion with my virgin milk shall regain innocence; he who has thus nourished himself shall then thirst at once for the seeds of my phallus; but he who drinks my seeds shall no longer even dream of invoking me, for he shall no longer be afraid of passing into the thousands of modifications that will never drain the Being."

"O give! That I may never need to invoke you again!"

"But woe betide him who with his memory drinks from my phallus for having spit upon my virgin breasts! For he drinks his own damnation!"

"O Baphomet! I hunger, I thirst for your milk, your seeds, do not let me languish like a parched stag!" whispered the gusting oblivion of the Grand Master, prowling about the swollen bodice of the breasts of the enclosed nun.

"Do you renounce your charge as Grand Master?"

"I've never had such a charge, as far as I know; but since you claim that I have, I renounce it heartily!"

"Do you promise me not to celebrate the anniversary of your torture any longer, as you have done for centuries?"

"I do not know that I was ever tortured, except by you and your questions! I shall celebrate nothing but your name!"

"Do you accept to be effaced from the memories of men as well as from your own?"

"What is my memory? Who was I? Who am I? Who shall I be? Baphomet, succour me quickly!"

"What do you wish?"

"All the modifications!"

"Look!"

And the nun indicated before her the figure of a kneeling, old man, hands clasped, eyes closed, mouth agape.

"Who is that?" asked the Grand Master's gusting oblivion.

"The memory of Sir Jacques de Molay, who is opposed to my nurturing your oblivion!"

"What does it want, to remain before you thus in prayer?"

"It wants its Creator to remember his attitude at his resurrection: it scorns the oblivion that flows from my virgin breasts as much as it desires the same from my phallus."

"What? Would it drink its own damnation?"

"That's not the reason it thirsts for my seeds, but to nourish itself with insult, though it be damned for it: for indeed, he who drinks me with his memory insults me, O oblivious breath who remembers my warnings all too well!"

"Why do you submit to the insults of memory, O you who dispense oblivion?"

"Because insult causes my seeds to flow! Thus does the Prince of Modifications of Being delight in his own modification!"

"Could it be that insult modifies you yourself in oblivion?"

"It is necessary in order to satisfy the Creator! Do I not myself insult his creation! He consents to his creatures' insulting me in exchange: therein lies their merit, which He remembers! While I myself forget that I ever took pleasure in it! Now keep a prudent distance while I discharge myself of my duties to your memory!"

"How then may I adore you in my oblivion, so that you will keep your promise?"

"Be faithful in your oblivion, down to the very last insult!"

"O Baphomet, don't let me languish!"

"I say in truth that before you have tasted me, you will have denied me three times!"

"Never, I swear!"

"Will you even remember having thus sworn!"

And so saying, the young nun approached the figure of the kneeling old man.

"Call me a sorceress, play-actress and bitch again! You may say it without fear! Am I not excluded from the circle of the elect?"

"Yes, of course!" cried the old man, keeping his eyes still closed, his hands clasped.—"Yes, and I am pleased to know you thus excluded!"

With these words the veiled figure's wimple split open with the top of the bodice, and the breasts of a maiden emerged. But far from keeping his distance, the Grand Master's oblivious breath, whirling and raising the veil, spread itself across the bared chest. Once the figure of the being thus modified had summoned his memory, the reply echoed in his own oblivion.

"Assuredly you are nothing but a sorceress!" shouted the old man, so forcefully that the wrathful breath that bore this utterance caused it to spiral towards the fringe of the black robe: slipping underneath, the words whirled in the shadow along the boyish legs sheathed in breeches and then lost their way.

"You shall burn for all eternity with the fire that sustains your shame!" belched the old man.

At this curse the nun reeled, spreading her palms as if looking for a support in the emptiness, and did not

104

regain her equilibrium until she had opened to the Grand Master's oblivious breath the path to irrevocable wrong.

"Ah, she sighed, her visage crimson, "now you ransack my sorceress' shame! Is that why you scorned my virgin breasts? Why not take your ingratitude further and deny that I'm an actress! Stop returning to the past! What? . . . You insist?"

At that moment, down around her lower belly, her gown seemed to rise lightly, puckering as though around a ball.

But the figure of the kneeling old man, eyes still closed, suddenly separated his folded hands and brought his right hand to the hem of the long gown, which he violently hoisted above the nun's sash: between the silken breeches there appeared, ridiculous and swollen, the satin codpiece of the youth, who still wore the nun's cornet on his head.

"You, so perfectly assured that your votive statue bears witness to your virginity to the heavens," thundered Sir Jacques de Molay's memory again, "you don't even hesitate to simulate manhood among us! What can I call you if not a consummate actress!"

The codpiece split open. In haste the nun covered the flagrancy with her palm, allowing her veil to fall.

"Though you have discovered my actress's ploy," she replied, her flow rising with the growing oblivion, "that doesn't make me a bitch for it! Come on, my Lord, give it one last try!"

"Bitch! Have I not said enough?" protested the memory of Sir Jacques, eyes still closed, hands folded again, his mouth remaining agape.

"O fecund malice!" answered the deaf whisper of the Grand Master's oblivious breath, unable to reach the goal of its exploration.

105

Then, insulted to his liking by the memory, though explored in full by the oblivion, his palm already moistening with an ingenuous agitation, the young boy cried:

"You who failed to nourish yourself with the virgin milk of a sorceress, drink a bitch's seeds from the phallus of a play-actress!" He shuddered, stripped of his veils. "Ha! It's done, Sir Jacques!"

Gushing from under his palm, the seeds, clouding the diamond on his finger, fell into the memory's gaping mouth.

Sir Jacques de Molay, having completed his prayer of thanksgiving, opened his eyes:

Beneath the high vault, at the end of a rope, hung the nude body of Ogier de Beauséant.

"Baphomet, Baphomet, why hast thou forsaken me?" howled the Grand Master.

At his cries, the window that gave onto the interior of the room opened, and the King appeared in his Templar's robe.

"Sir Jacques," he whispered, "Is that an initiation to the second or the third degree?"

VIII

" . . . Beware, my Brethren; into what kind of truth
have you fallen?" . . . The slow or sudden destruction
of the body—I say body out of deference to humanity—
destruction through misfortune or violence, never fails
to bear upon the breath: shall one blame it for its right
to recover its freedom, a right it has been granted? Is it
conceivable that, if the breath has always had a ten-
dency to quit this body, abuse it or make it an accomplice to its ultimate destruction, it should not now feel
its effects? Be on your guard, my Brethren! From here
it is but one step to say that everything a breath has
perpetrated through its body—I mean through its
dissimulation—could remain without consequence
once it has left this body, thus bearing no trace of this
dissimulation—since we differ in no wise from the
winds or air currents, even when they bring malice or
sensual craving to infect other places! Yet what can we
say of the violence of one breath toward another? Can
the latter condemn the first for having destroyed its

107

fragile habitation, when it should be free of all need to remain the same? What have I not witnessed in this respect during the exercise of my charge! I should not go so far as to say that the victim breath no longer recognizes its victimizer. Rather, it seems to seek further outrage, if not from a need to know that it exists, then at least to prove to itself the futility of the wrong it has suffered. But the flight that brings the suddenly expired breaths to us does not grant them time enough to realize this: relieved of the need to remain the same, the victim breaths merge with the victimizers once they see them coming. The latter seem not to know the shame of seeing themselves thus welcomed by the others. No accusations or regrets on either side, and no forgiveness. Except that the former victimizers will be weaker than their former victims if ever they should seek to separate from them. There is no moral atonement here, and such could hardly be required. A violence of another order is born of our condition: it is effected by means of a total indifference. It is this indifference itself: and it leaves no trace, which is the worst form of violence! Against this I must struggle, my Brethren, until the resurrection of the flesh.''

As these last words are still resonating, the guests sit down to table with a joyous tumult and lean towards each other, emulously addressing and challenging one another; the ranks of the pages disperse; platters are passed around, wine flows in abundance; nevertheless, one guest cannot get over his astonishment; he makes an effort not to betray his uneasiness, squints at his neighbor, the Visitor of the Order, who smiles at him courteously, but—might the Visitor also be concealing some perplexity?—parts his lips only for a draught or a bite: for there is no want of appetite—if only, as the Grand Master said, out of deference to humanity.

This guest, now completely bewildered, is Brother Damiens, the fortress's new Chaplain: having arrived with the Visitor the previous evening, he spent the entire night hearing the confession of each of the Brethren knights; in the darkness it seemed to him that it was always the same voice accusing itself of greater and greater transgressions, and when he hastened to absolve them on the condition that they perform the moderate penance he assigned them, the voices returned to him to beg harsher penances. At dawn, he celebrated Mass in a completely empty chapel, while whispers reiterated this response: *I was taken for him who I am not.*

Why did the Grand Master express himself so circuitously? Could it be that the separated souls have the privilege of embracing truth or falsehood according to their moods, and that perchance they pass themselves off as dead? All these men, so fresh and vigorous in appearance, are bursting with health, the old no less than those in their prime and those whose cheeks are lightly covered with down. But—and such is what confuses Brother Damiens—all manifest an extraordinary flexibility, a disturbing suppleness: standing or seated, they seem as if suspended; in moving about, they glide rather than walk; first they bounce with hurried steps, then float slowly; sometimes they appear frozen in a gesture, hues and volumes accentuating one another; at other times everything accelerates, colors blur or overflow their contours. They whisper; then a burst of laughter escapes and spreads into a reddish stain, turning violet, then azure; at last distinct words begin to restore to each his physiognomy; then an objection, a doubt, a hypothesis are put forth, unwinding and unfurling in long velvet folds; they caress the details of embroidered gold and hasten to draw out the pearly cloak; first the folds are smoothed and the cross lies radiant on the linen, then its limbs break on the crumpled cloth and coil around an arm in sinuous petals.

At this moment, the call of a horn sounds in the distance, and everyone rushes to the transom windows of the refectory.

On the heights of the hills, along their slopes and into the valley crowded a throng of bareheaded horsemen with sparkling breast-plates. Tied with fillets, their hair streamed in the wind.

One of them, mounted on a black charger, began to prance as he hugged the moat, contemplating the high walls; he shook a burning torch which he then threw towards the central window out of which leaned the Visitor of the Order, the Seneschal and, standing slightly back, the Grand Master. Suddenly the torch stops in mid-air at the level of their faces, and its flames part: at its center appears a man's head crowned with a papal tiara; opening its mouth, it exclaims: "It is to convey to you their warning, O Sir Jacques, our dearly beloved son, that the Thrones and Dominions have momentarily drawn us from the fire in which our souls are cleansed of pusillanimity to protect you from iniquity! Forgive Clement, unworthy servant of God's servants! But if you have any pity for a conscience consumed by sorrow and nourished by hope, listen! Thus speak the heavenly powers: 'Of two things you must choose one: Either you shall celebrate the anniversary of your torment with a clear conscience, and we shall confer an intelligible consistency upon your memory and upon that of your Brethren for the time of this solemn ceremony, as a promise of future glory—but in that case, O Grand Master of the Temple, do not admit spirits that deny that God ever created natures eternally identical to themselves and responsible for their acts and thoughts! For one such spirit has slipped into your fortress to seduce the expired breaths and to show them that there is no unity and that nothing stays forever the same but that all changes perpetually until all combinations are exhausted and the cycle recommences indefinitely in an innocence as hopeless as it is absurd; this spirit has taken on the shape of a mammal from unexplored lands: beware that it does not pass itself off as heraldic and become the blazon of the Holy Order! Renounce your multiplication of the rites and emblems, lest you become the first victim of your too obvious ruses! Or if you think you can use your breath with impunity to insufflate exalted spirits into bodies in dormition at the expense of the souls separated from these and of the bodies themselves, go then conspire with blind powers and ask them to sustain your rash spiration! But expect nothing from us! Be therefore vigilant in your holy ministry and cease to grant asylum to him who said that: *all the gods died of laughter to hear one among them proclaim himself unique!* You know of whom we speak: If before dawn you have not delivered to us Frederick the Antichrist, who has come among you in the guise of an anteater, as the sun is rising over the newly dying we shall chase you from your fortress and drive you to the lower circles of your forever futile past! Woe betide him who would perjure himself as many times as there are dwellings in the house of the Father!' This, O Grand Master, is what the Thrones and Dominions say to you! Pray for my wretched soul, alleviate my so deserved sufferings!"

The last words vanished into the crackling of the

torch, which fell back into the hands of the young horseman. Shaking it several times, he galloped away, rejoining the host before him, where hair streamed like oriflammes over the armor and the motionless steeds.

The Grand Master followed him with his gaze for a long time, then turning towards his intimates:

"What a strange way of exhorting us to vigilance, showing us the repentant soul of Clement—at the end of a torch! presumably lighted in Purgatory! To dissuade me from multiplying the rites and emblems when they themselves use them with might and main! No! The Thrones and Dominions speak more directly! What was he trying to say? An anteater, was it? What have I to do with Frederick? Hohenstaufen, no doubt? The Antichrist . . . an anteater? I, perjure myself? What mockery! Chase me from my fortress? . . . Fear not, my Brethren," he said, extending his arms to a group of knights whom he saw giving orders to the valets-at-arms, "no rash replies now; let no man move or leave! Come, let us be seated again and continue the discussion! Brother Damiens, where were we?"

The Grand Master, followed by a throng of guests, had resumed his place at the long table of the dignitaries.

At the far end of the vast hall, foreigners, merchants, pilgrims and a few ladies admitted as an exception on that day, due to the solemnity of the occasion, had waited for him to sit down before making themselves comfortable and resuming their chatter, entirely unaware of the miraculous summons. As for the dignitaries of the Order who, surrounding the Grand Master, had witnessed it, although each of them interpreted in his own fashion the words uttered—for none failed to apply them to himself—at present each recalled only the formulation of an incomprehensible demand for extradition, followed by threats.

Twenty or so Brethren knights, armed from head to foot, remained standing around their Grand Master. Turning towards them he proclaimed:

"It is not the first time, as you are well aware, that we have been disturbed at this late hour! Certainly it is not to be discounted that this may be some new ruse of Philip's . . . or rather . . . a last bitter taste of his anger at not being admitted to the third degree! . . . It's too old a story! Perhaps he's in the process of redrafting for the thousandth time the account of our affair, and the ideas are becoming confused in the mind of the scribe whose lucubrations, for want of information about our secrets, are now the cause of all these threats: but they cannot burn us twice!" With these words he seized the handle of his goblet, then added:

"I . . . insufflate spirits into bodies in dormition! . . . Who has ever encountered a body here? . . ."

Suddenly, an adolescent's hand, holding a ewer, fills the Grand Master's goblet to the brim, then pours a drink for the Brother knight across from him. The youth withdraws his arm and resumes his place behind the knight, among the other children. He seems to be the youngest, and keeps his eyes lowered. The Grand Master is struck by the purity of his features and his grace of bearing.

"Who is it that just served us?" he asks Brother Lahire de Champsceaux.

"My lord, that is the Lord of Beauséant, a noble orphan; his aunt, Lady of Palençay, great grand-niece of our illustrious benefactor Jean de Saint-Vit, after rearing him tenderly, hath entrusted him to our care."

"The sight of him brings us great joy, Brother Lahire! Is he a good child?"

"Timid but brave, and most able in the heat of the fray!"

"What say ye there, Brother knight! Is he even of age to assume the rank of squire?"

" . . . An ye break three lances," Lahire continues, "he will give you yet a fourth, though ye weened yourself dead or at the enemy's mercy! And were ye to waste two steeds withal, he were there straightaway to the rescue, to put you in the saddle of his own! If he takes the eternal vows of our Temple, I shall make him my gift to you!"

"Gramercy! I drink to you both!"

Hardly have they emptied their cups at this proposal when, seated a little farther away between the Visitor and the Seneschal, one of the dignitaries rises: should not the Grand Master have already recognized him as the Commander of Saint-Vit, he too a guest at this solemn repast? Pale and standing, shaking his head incessantly, he leaves the table and, almost reeling, proceeds towards the opposite end of the hall, disappearing from sight. Why does the Grand Master breathe more easily now? He detests this breath that opened up before him like an abyss: but when? Something thereafter remains nonetheless, modifying them each in turn, mutually.

And so an adolescent's hand, the same as always, again pours him a drink, a hand with tapered fingers on which shines a diamond. The young boy is there, behind the chair of Brother Lahire, facing the Grand Master and the new Chaplain seated to the right of Sir Jacques; farther away, between the Visitor and the

114

Seneschal, sits the Commander . . . . The situation is the same: Ogier has once more joined the ranks of the pages, his elders. The Grand Master will notice anon the purity of his traits, the grace of his bearing; already he turns to ask Lahire: "Who is it that served us? . . ."

But an eternity is reflected in the waters of the diamond on the page's ring, which now cuts through the Grand Master's eternity: at this moment he speaks as if never having lived on this earth was for him, the Grand Master, his essential condition.

He stopped himself and raised the goblet to his lips, but put it back down without having drunk:

"Who among us has ever encountered a body? . . . Here . . . where we are all but smoke . . . for how much longer still? . . . It's certainly been long enough to know how matters stand . . . . And for what purpose has the King of the Two Sicilies come here? He who once so detested us, would he now seek refuge among us? Perhaps after our trial we suddenly became likeable to him? It has been a long time since I informed the whirlwinds: and had I perceived and recognized him, may God damn me if I would ever have refused him hospitality! . . . And yet," he said into the new chaplain's ear, "I did refuse that rascal Philip . . . Perhaps he resents me for having informed him . . . I let him whirl his fill, blow with a fury between the walls and tapestries . . ." and, raising his voice: "Perhaps we breathe him now!" Then, looking at the guests nearest him:

"Obviously, one cannot separate one breath from the next, far from it, and many breaths united make a lot of wind; thus if one wants to isolate them and to concentrate on one of them by creating a vacuum for it, which cannot happen unless one retains one's own breath, the one that one wished to extricate from the

115

others is not always the first to emerge, and one is never sure of recovering oneself afterwards! But . . . an anteater? An anteater? I ask you, young men, do our stables house any other species besides horses and camels? Could it have gone to the depths of the old cellar? Ogier, what do you think? Ogier, answer me!"

But Ogier had disappeared.

"What!" exclaimed the Grand Master, "Ogier has slipped away without our permission!" And, beside himself, he rose: "Ogier!" he shouted, making the high vaults reverberate, and rushing to the middle of the hall and running to the opposite table: "But why weren't you watching him, Brother Gauvain!" So saying he grabbed the beard of the keeper of the pages.

"You know very well of whom I speak! Ogier," he said in a trembling voice, "the boy barely fourteen years of age!"

And with his hand he indicated the boy's height in the air.

" . . . and you allow the youngest of your youths to run about these uncertain places!"

Brother Gauvain vainly indicated the fifty boys who, at the cries of the Grand Master, had come running from the four corners of the refectory and forthwith crowded about their keeper.

"They are all here, my Lord Grand Master," said Gauvain, eyes bulging, a beseeching look on his face. "Fifty of them: not one is missing. Ogier is not in my care," and he turned towards the children who, with zeal, cried in unison: "Ogier is not one of us!"

Meanwhile Brother Damiens, the new confessor, gazed at them; he still hadn't seen Ogier, and thus did not understand the Grand Master's distress; but to see these children so tenderly intertwined, some climbing on others' shoulders, agile, cajoling and enticing,

116

forming arabesques of interlacing arms and legs, sparkling undulations of black hair and blond, brows knit and velvet eyes scampish, astonished or amused, vermillion mouths half-open or whistling, hands applauding or snapping their fingers, or forming slender fists against their hips and elbowing one another—to see this shuffling, tittering lot abruptly fall silent, he said to himself: *"Here are the Thrones and Dominions!"*

"Ogier is not one of us!" the young boys cried once more; then the joyous swarm scattered back to the four corners of the hall and each boy returned to his duties.

Supported by Brother Gauvain, the Grand Master, gasping for air, returned to the dignitaries' table. They saw him turn pale: "Ah, God! I should have known!" he said, dropping into his chair.

He made as if to form the syllables of a name, wasting his breath in trying to free them from their impenetrable depths: his utterance remained incoherent.

In this hall where he was celebrating the day of his torment surrounded by his table companions, several of whom had perished with him, he could only explore those figures who were contemporaneous with his lifetime. But how might this name, which had arisen in an epoch subsequent to his own and had only come to his knowledge thanks to his wanderings outside of his fortress, have properly lent itself to invocation? Having expelled and then buried its first designation inside himself, he could only conceive of it now as the absent visage of the young boy who had remained silent to his call.

Everyone here, at every table from end to end, knew one another and spoke in familiar terms, as though all that had happened centuries ago were now about to happen again. He himself was not supposed to know

Beauséant; but contrary to all expectation, he had clamored for him loudly, and the more he had insisted on the fact of Ogier's disappearance, the greater the surprise he had aroused; all the same, had not Ogier just poured them drinks? Yet Lahire breathed not a word, the Commander paid no mind to his consternation, and Gauvain, keeper of the pages, and his troop of boys denied knowing Beauséant. There was a reason for such behavior, and this too belonged to the past. Now, as though unwittingly disobeying an order, the Grand Master had effected the recurrence of the already transpired through a process that remained obscure to him. Was he celebrating the anniversary of his torment, or was he foretelling it? At that moment, it became impossible to distinguish whether the disappearance of Ogier, of whose presence no one had any suspicion, presented itself as a new development, or whether, on the contrary, monastic custom demanded that the Brethren knights display a tacit ignorance.

Suddenly three sharp blows of a halberd ring out: all fall silent. The guests rise, all eyes turned towards the entrance; but the knights standing opposite the Grand Master turn their backs to the group of people who, from the back of the hall, are making their way to the dignitaries' table: it's the King himself, in the company of several nobles; he gestures for all to be seated; no one moves. Philip, dressed in the robe of the Temple, comes forward like a simple Brother knight, bowing before the Grand Master. Remaining seated and looking distracted, Sir Jacques de Molay pays not the least bit of attention to the King.

"Thank you," says Philip, "thank you for your hospitality, my Lord Grand Master, you whom the spirit of submission to God moves to cast a veil of largesse over your austerity! The rabble have been brought to reason, we take our leave with regret: this holy house affords a solid rampart to our persons, body and soul! We hereby place this banquet to our credit. The rest we shall share among Brethren. We shall see to the tithe. And we await you, Lord Grand Master, at the funeral of our daughter-in-law." And tapping him on the shoulder:

"Sir Jacques, to your health!"

The King drinks in long draughts from the Grand Master's goblet. The latter, eyes fixed, does not even make a show of rising or of inclining his head to acknowledge his farewell . . .

The same scene unfolds each time Sir Jacques sits down to table with his Brethren to celebrate the anniversary of his torment: does he know or does he not that the King has never and will never fail to request asylum at the Temple on the eve of the anniversary of the torment and that, the better to disturb the commemorative repast, not having been invited, he unfailingly will come to take his leave of the Grand Master? The entrance of the King is inseparable from this commemoration: but as Philip's remarks and gestures are repeated, the ritual cheer of the repast makes them seem more discourteous; as the Grand Master awaits their recurrence, he yields to his historical vexation and becomes frozen in it, excluding Philip's gestures and remarks from the ritual of the meal. Yet through his very attitude does not Sir Jacques exclude himself as well?

Actually, the Grand Master, to all appearances deaf to Philip's words, watches, each time the scene repeats itself, for what the King will tell him anew: from eternity to eternity the same provocations arise: "We place this banquet to our credit! We await you at the funeral or our daughter-in-law. To your health, Sir Jacques!" But—was it always so, or is this the first time?—as Sir Jacques de Molay remains petrified with resentment, Philip now whispers into his ear:

"Have you considered admitting me at last to the second degree? The stake that I ignited on that unfortunate day burns eternally! And your perversity shall prosper for eternity! Therein lies the fruit of wrong committed upon your innocence! But what is innocence uninjured? Baphomet is well worth his weight in gold!"

Hardly has he heard those three syllables when, exhaling in a moan from the mouth of Sir Jacques, his memory evaporates and his historical vexation is inhaled by the King. Heavy with his own offense, Philip falls to his knees before the Grand Master. Forthwith the latter regains his lightness and leans towards the King:

"What's come over you, Brother Philip? A long time has passed since I retracted my retraction at the stake! What I claimed freely to believe was false; what I admitted under torture without belief, I see here as truth! Down there you were wrong to burn me, here you are right to do so! Stand up!"

"I've had enough of being right! Command the ordeals!"

Then, upon a sign from the Grand Master, a large golden bowl is passed to the King, which he holds in his hands.

A voice resounds:

"Philip, our Brother, what do you offer the Grand Master?"

"My head," replies the King.

"Why do you wish to die yet again, instead of eating

120

and drinking among us? One dies but once, yet one never finishes eating and drinking among Brethren!"

"I destroyed the Temple!"

"May you be forgiven, Brother Philip! What more do you want?"

"To rebuild the Temple!"

"To what end?"

"To play dead among the living!"

Upon this, from the back of the hall, a figure veiled in black from head to foot comes forth; as like a lightning bolt flashing from a dark cloud, from a parting in the veils there springs a fine, white hand brandishing the gleaming blade of a scimitar; with one stroke the figure severs Philip's head and receives it in the bowl. Decapitated, the King presents it to the Grand Master. Severed, the head nonetheless speaks:

"Here is the pledge of my promise: I shall rebuild the Temple."

Then the Grand Master lifts the severed head from the bowl, gives it the kiss of peace, passes it to the other Brethren and thus, from hand to hand, the royal head makes its way around the long tables, at last returning to the hands of the veiled figure. The latter, grasping it by the hair, crosses to the center of the refectory, presents it to the company and making the sign of the cross raises it up and down, and from left to right. The guests cross themselves in turn. The same figure then conceals the royal head beneath its veils and waits, immobile.

At the Grand Master's feet, the still kneeling, head-less King has collapsed forward, hands upon the flag-stones. The Seneschal rings his bell. A voice resounds:

"Brother Philip, do you need your body?"

"Brethren," replies the severed head from beneath

the veils, "let no one reveal where I am! I'm slaking my hunger, let no one disturb me: not even my body!"

Meanwhile, at the other end of the refectory where the crowded throng of pilgrims, travellers and merchants is carousing, the people have witnessed the last peripeties of the rite and now, in a rage, the guilds and other corporations invade the space that separates them from the table of the dignitaries of the Order; indicating the prostrate King, they roar:

"Give us the counterfeiter!"

But already from another table a group of Jews come running and begin to crawl around the royal trunk, wailing in lamentation, beating their breasts and trying to raise the royal body to its feet. The guilds intervene and roar threateningly.

"Brother Philip, do you give your body to the Jews as you have left your head with us as a pledge?" asks the same voice.

"They won't get a sou for it!" replies the severed head from under the veils. "Throw my body into the Seine!"

The fifty young pages, taking no notice of the furious ringing of the Seneschal's bell, cry out in unison: "Brother Philip, stand up! Show us where your head is hiding! Come on, start looking!"

The trunk of the King suddenly raises itself and all stand back. He extends his arms before him, and keeping his balance, he stumbles to the Grand Master's table, seeking the hands of Sir Jacques.

"Do not soil your hand by touching mine, Grand Master!" protests the head from beneath the veils.

The beheaded King withdraws from the table, turns around and with arms outstretched continues its halting walk toward the middle of the room. But as he makes ready to turn his back to the veiled figure, the

122

Jews decide to support him and try to guide him: the artisans and merchants opposite them roar all the louder, though spellbound by his acephalic majesty, whom they dare not approach. Then slowly proceeding toward the side of those clamoring, the King with a rapid gesture detaches a whip from his belt and begins furiously to crack it left and right. Some move aside, some follow; some try to confuse him. The beheaded King stops, throws down his whip and untying a purse, scatters crowns into open hands.

"What actions you force me to take, O Grand Master! Open the cesspool, I beg you!" cries the head beneath the veils. "Keep me from returning to my body!"

The latter pursues his course: three steps from the veiled personage, as he was extending his hands, a flagstone gives way beneath his foot: the King slips and vanishes into a pit.

"Where has the counterfeiter gone?" cry the artisans.

"The Jews have conjured him away to sell him!" answer the merchants.

"Death to the Jews!"

Upon the latter, who were kissing the fatal flagstone, the mob hurl themselves pell-mell; and all topple into the pit, following the King.

At the tables the din is at its peak: laughing shamelessly, the Brethren knights themselves lose shape in the eyes of the terrified Brother Damiens; the Visitor of the Order turns, disturbed, toward the Grand Master: but deaf to this indecorous mirth, Sir Jacques keeps his eyes fixed upon the figure in long veils. The Seneschal does not cease to ring his bell, then with the handle of his sword he strikes hard upon the table.

With silence restored, the figure standing previously

immobile uncovers himself with a single gesture: only Brother Damiens is frozen in astonishment to recognize Philip intact from head to foot. The Brethren knights cross their arms. Once again surrounded by his nobles, the King speaks:

"O Grand Master and you, venerable Brethren, each of you here is free to use in his own manner the rites of this solemn ceremony. Does its repetition abolish the evil of the historical events? . . . Well, yes! Once again the rabble have been brought to reason! Once again we take our leave with regret! Once again deceit for deceit, my Brethren. Thus until next year you may breathe again this rascal breath! . . ."

While shaking with laughter his figure vanished into the penumbra; but his dying laughter only provoked the Grand Master's oblivion all the more.

"Did you not promise not to celebrate the anniversary of your torment any longer? No longer to commemorate my infamy? But to whom did you promise this?"

No sooner have these words dissolved into silence than shouts are raised from the other end of the hall. Travellers and pilgrims who were banqueting at the foot of the entrance pillars are now seen pressing against the doorways. The group of guards disperse this crowd and form a barrier, while Ogier, mounted on a furry monster that he guides with a chain, slowly advances through the rows of tables; there is not a single guest that does not detain him at each step to examine as closely as possible the animal whose diminutive head and long muzzle obstinately sliding along the flagstones contrast with the enormous body and paws armed with long claws. Gauvain's fifty pages are not the last to disturb its labored steps, unable to restrain themselves as they vie to pull the long hairs of its erect tail. With this tail, as with a broom, the monster thrashes the impish boys as it passes, driving them back in fright. Meanwhile the Brethren knights are no less astonished by the youth than by his monster. Squeezed inside his silken, white and black striped costume, his ebony hair falling in coils about his shoulders, he bends his fresh face forward, lowering his long-lashed eyelids; his vermillion, half-parted lips smile in satisfaction, his glowing cheeks seem painted; his chest gives off a strange scent that mingles with the foul odor of the beast; he removes his gloves and with his slender hands he strokes the monster, having arrived at last at the table of the dignitaries; with one movement of his supple form, he leaps from the monster's back; suddenly the astonished Grand Master finds Ogier before him. The squire kneels, stands up and in the tone of someone resuming a recently interrupted discussion, he declares:

"Strange caprice! He refuses ants."

"From whence have you returned?" stammers Sir Jacques. Much more moved by the sound of that sweet voice in his ear than surprised by the suspicious presence of the anteater, he has to conceal his joy beneath an appearance of consternation:

"But where did you find it?" Then regaining possession of himself: "Now then! If it was really within our walls," he said, "who brought it here without forewarning us? But then," and he cast a glance towards the window, "they are still waiting . . . I see nothing any more!! Could it be true? . . . My Brethren, shall we call the Chapter together?"

"Then you might as well surrender, Grand Master," intervened the Visitor of the Order. "When all your Brethren are ready to defend this place . . . to convene the Chapter is to cast doubt on your position." All the dignitaries murmured in approval.

"My position? . . . From the moment I inform an expired breath I allow it to come and go here as it pleases: I neither pursue it nor simply keep it hostage. But if I thus respect the laws of hospitality, am I also responsible for the animal aspects that may have once inspired or might still inspire a past or future spirit? Shall I too be attributed the appearance of a bronze mountain on the horizon or the disproportion of a tree with its hideous foliage? What can I do against the whims of a Throne or Dominion that wishes to amuse itself independently? Its peers know they can restrain it no more than they can restrain us. Shall they therefore make us modify the purpose of this fortress or constrain us to abandon it for another? The attack with which they threaten us amounts to nothing more than a formality. For the eternities in which we have resided here, the lower and upper Circles have seemed to tolerate each other without encroachment. For a conspiracy of this sort to come batter our walls and call our jurisdiction into question, we must assume that some disturbance—I know not what—has occurred in the economy of the spheres . . ."

With these words, the Grand Master let his gaze wander to the mammal and from the mammal to Ogier. The latter was conspicuously contemplating the crucifix hanging from a chain around the Grand Master's neck, then he began to stare at the old man, eye to eye.

Then suddenly:

"Let us treat it like a postulant and it will reveal its true nature to us. Several Brethren knights shall form a circle around us as we sit in this small oratory. You, Ogier, shall keep our guest at the threshold while we interrogate it from our seats before the altar."

All approached a small ogival arch which opened, doorless, onto a small chapel where at times the Grand Master used to retire to collect himself after meals.

127

"Shall we subject it to the test of spitting on the crucifix?" asked some.

"Who has ever really understood this test of spitting?" retorted the Visitor of the Order.

"Would it even do it, if it was really Hohenstaufen?" objected the Seneschal.

"In that case no test would be valid for this unbeliever," replied the Grand Master. "The purpose of the test is to confuse, in appearance, willing consent with the constraint of performing a hateful act. For what does spitting on the instrument of our salvation represent materially? That we refuse to be saved! Now, he who uses the test to spit deliberately, deems himself comfortable in perdition. On the other hand, he who ardently hopes to be saved body and soul also believes with all his might in the grace of Christ's passion. If in spite of this ardent desire to be saved he forces himself to spit upon the Savior and willfully consents not to distinguish himself in any manner from one who spits deliberately, he suffers with the Savior and does so in Trinitarian fashion: he suffers with the Father when he denied his own son in his humanity upon the cross; with the Son in his humanity thus denied; and with the Holy Spirit that the Father withdrew from him. But is not the Holy Spirit the Spirit of both? Did not the Holy Spirit suffer by denying Himself? . . ."

"But how, in all seriousness, can one lay so deceptive a trap for a human soul sunken to the bestial form that we see here?" the new Chaplain could not refrain himself from interjecting. "Could it ever see through the ruse enough to turn it to its own advantage? Do you not want it to affirm the incarnation by denying it?"

"The incarnation?" bellowed the Grand Master,

128

and with his fist he dealt a powerful blow to the slender spine of Brother Damiens. "The incarnation! That's not what interests us here! Our concern is to know all that a bodiless breath is capable of, to go so far as to assume this distressing form: Might this be its beatitude which thus appears before our eyes, or rather could it be a pleasure still bestial after it has been appropriated by a spirit? If our postulant is indeed Frederick of Sicily, he should be perfectly comfortable with spitting; and all the more so if what we have before us is a simple mammal! How is one to distinguish, then, the real supposite of such a state? Does this mean that as a mammal of unknown species Frederick is worse off than in the throes of eternal punishment? Or would his spirit do less harm in this form, and humbly work towards the universal good simply because it is an anteater and not the Holy Roman Emperor? Unless in his human form he had an anteater's soul . . . . Let us hope for some sign of malaise, to assure us of the presence of another agent!"

With these words, the Grand Master sat down on the steps of the altar; the dignitaries and the Chaplain remained at his sides. Ten knights, backs turned to the refectory to hide the scene from the sight of the people, surrounded Ogier and his animal.

The anteater appeared to want to enter the chapel as well, and tugged on the chain, which Ogier let fall. The Visitor of the Order blocked his way. But the Grand Master asked "Is it not his right? Let him be." Then:

"What do you want?"

Forthwith, the anteater raised its tiny head and as much as its prodigiously long claws in front and back would allow, it tried to prostrate itself at the feet of the Grand Master. More amused than moved by these efforts, which appeared to express a humble request for mercy, Sir Jacques asked the young page: "Could you already have tamed it so well?" And leaning towards the beast:

"What do you seek?"

As everyone was curiously waiting to see by what other pose it would express the very thing with which no one here concerned himself, being all too certain of possessing it already—"eternal life," that is—the anteater, unsteady on its four paws, began to turn in circles with lowered head, dragging its long snout along the flagstones and shaking its long-haired tail, which was raised in the air like a flag. It seemed as if it would never stop, when the Grand Master, removing the crucifix from his neck, laid it across the beast's path.

Three times in succession the circles slowly described by the anteater brought it to the crucifix lying on the ground, and each time that it struck against it with its snout the Grand Master asked, "Do you know who this is?" Whether or not it had understood, the animal extended its tensile tongue and smeared the Savior's image with its spittle before casting it behind itself with its long-clawed paw. Following the same circular path, the animal drew away from it, as far as the chapel's entrance. Now dragging its chain around Ogier, it retraced its steps and, following the same circuit, snout assiduously lowered to the ground, it came across the crucifix again; and having wet it once more with its long tongue and cast it away, it was already resuming its never-ending round when, from the back of the refectory where a few lingering pilgrims of low birth were feasting, one of them, overcome with drink, screamed at the top of his lungs:

Cock-a-doodle-do![1] At the very same moment, with its entire body standing on its hind legs, the anteater raised its front paws, striking and shredding the air with its claws, shook its small head and let itself fall upon the crucifix; its whole hairy mass rolling itself into a ball, it hid its head beneath its long claws, covering its snout.

"Sir Jacques," said the Visitor of the Order, "these rustics are all we needed to complete the clown show."

"Whether the cock crows of itself or from the throat of a drunk, matters little here!" answered the Grand Master.

"I was unaware that the cock's crowing was indispensable to the test of spitting!" observed the new Chaplain.

"That's because you have never spit," retorted a knight.

"Place any hard inedible object in its path, large or small, this dagger for example, and it will spit on it in the same fashion!" said the Visitor.

"But you did not think of that before! This idea occurs to you only now! The beast circled around Christ Crucified, not around just any object!"

"If it stood up, it's because the cry of that ruffian frightened it!" persisted the Visitor and, leaning over the prostrate anteater, since he could not make out any ear, he shouted: "Cock-a-doodle-do! Cock-a-doodle-do!"

But far from shifting its position, the anteater only hoisted its enormous tail higher and, coiling it over its

---

[1]In the original text, Klossowski's onomatopoeic cock's crow, *Qui que rit qui!*, is a pun that means literally "Whoever laughs who," and plays on the laughter of the gods cited in this chapter and above.

hairy back, unfurled the extremity's long mane and appeared to screen itself from the wrong they had done it by questioning its behavior.

"Can you not see it is overcome by what it has just done!" insisted the Grand Master. "I cannot overlook this appearance: consider at least what it expresses! For, in fact—except for the state of indifference, which is our own, whence all of this comes—of two things, one must be true: either it feels guilty and we should be equally so not to impute its guilt accordingly—or else it's an impostor! In either case, this anteater is very well informed!"

"But then," said the Visitor, "this mob would be equally guilty for laughing at its expense!"

"Do you still believe in the secret, my Brother? Am I ever sure of whom I shelter here? But we must make an end of this!"

And addressing the anteater:

"Your repentance moves us! In spite of appearances, your nature is endowed with reason. This is why I exhort you, in the name of Him whose image you cast away and whom you now hide beneath you, to let us understand the truth: thus clad in this monstrous body, whether by choice or by a fate of which I am unaware, might you be Frederick Hohenstaufen, our old enemy?"

The anteater slowly relaxed itself, disengaged its small head and raised it towards the Grand Master, then seemed suddenly shaken by a violent shudder that ruffled the long hair of its enormous body.

"It's laughing in turn," said Ogier. "That is its way of laughing!"

This brusque intervention by the young page, who had been silent until then, drew glances of surprise. Had they forgotten that it was he who had discovered the animal and brought it to the refectory? Now he even took it upon himself to explain its conduct.

"Indeed," said the Seneschal, "should we not have questioned Lord Ogier?"

This was precisely what the Grand Master had wished to avoid at all costs; and so he hastened to press the matter further with the anteater.

"If you can understand me, let us know if you are or are not the Emperor Frederick, King of the Two Sicilies!"

Then the anteater—and one could not tell if it was or was not the voice of the young boy that passed through the beast's long, narrow snout—hissed:

"You have said it, I am King."

All turned around towards the page, for although it could not be proved that he had uttered those dominical words, still it seemed at least plausible that he had suggested them. The Grand Master was trembling, but nevertheless exclaimed:

"Come now, Ogier, will you keep silent at last? Brethren," he said to the knights, "see to it that Beauséant does not open his mouth!" And turning to the anteater:

"Are you aware that forces are besieging us which demand that I deliver Frederick the Antichrist to them?"

"I was once called Frederick," continued the anteater, once more borrowing the voice of the young boy. "But not the one you think!"

Since Ogier had made not a sound with his own voice, no one could understand how it could resonate so clearly in the monster's gullet. And although the Visitor of the Order was losing patience—imagining that the child was a ventriloquist, he was about to place his ear against his stomach—the Grand Master thought to spare himself this demonstration and signaled to Ogier to come and sit next to him. The page, shaking his long hair with a smiling, triumphant expression, took his place beside him; and leaning on his elbows on the second step of the altar, he rested his temple against Sir Jacques' knee. The latter had slipped his hand into the boy's hair, and while noticing that Lahire continued to stare at Ogier more than he had reason to, he continued his interrogation:

"Answer me without fear: since you are not Frederick Hohenstaufen, the alleged Antichrist they demand, it cannot be the Thrones and Dominions that besiege us. Rest assured, I shall not give you over to them, and if they hold it against your kingdom, I shall fight on your behalf!"

"My own kingdom is not of this world: if it were, all the anteaters of the world would come and fight on my behalf! I am not the king of the anteaters!"

"Do not blaspheme! Undoubtedly you are before us in such a state to expiate your impieties towards Him who spoke thus for our redemption!"

"I am the way, the truth and the life!"

"Once again, do not blaspheme, Frederick!"

"I am the Antichrist! and all that Christ says, so says the Antichrist at the same time! The words differ in no respect! One cannot tell them apart until after their respective consequences!"

"What consequences will follow your own? If you are the Antichrist, perform a miracle for the perdition of the elect! There are none here as far as I know . . ."

"As far as you know? . . . O Grand Master! If you do not want to be driven from your fortress yourself, you will hand me over! For I repeat to you: I am the way, the truth and the life!"

"Upon my honor, you shall remain our guest and our Brother! And I shall cure you of this notion of being the Antichrist! As for the besiegers, I await them undaunted!"

"Doubt not that it is the Thrones and Dominions who told you why they are besieging you and why they seek my extradition!"

"Why? They accuse you of having once said, at the sight of a field of wheat: *How many gods grow here!*"

"That's not what they told you about me, O Grand Master, your historical memory is evading the issue! I said more than that! Come now, remember!"

"What then did you say, something worse?"

The anteater was again overcome by the shudder that Ogier had interpreted as its way of laughing, but to demonstrate that this conjecture was not at all unfounded, it no longer spoke in the childish voice of the young boy, but in bursts of a sepulchral voice:

"When one god proclaimed himself unique, all the other gods died of laughter!"

"Do you dare to mock?" the suddenly furious Grand Master cried. "Leave that form at once, vile sorcerer!"

The anteater raised its diminutive head and, tilting it to the side, said: "Sorcerer? You are one as much as I!"

And it began to lick Ogier's hand.

Other Brethren knights crowded against the door of the small oratory. They heard only the questions asked; no one understood a word of the answers, but only guessed at them after each new question. Some said the Grand Master was amusing himself with Ogier; but the group of knights who for several moments had been observing the attitude of the young page had quite a different impression: Ogier was visibly following the dialogue in silence, and they were convinced that in order for the anteater to have so perfectly reproduced his childish voice, one same spirit must have been circulating between the two.

"Who is this jackanapes tied to that hairy monster like a thief to his accomplice?" they asked one another. "Look how he tolerates that horrible tongue and has no fear of its repulsive touch! Might it not be a trap set for us by the besiegers? Look at Sir Jacques so pale and covered with sweat! And Brother Damiens sits silent and does not move!" And they cast stealthy, troubled glances at the new confessor of the Temple. The latter, eyes half-closed, revealing nothing of his feelings—for indeed, all these palpable physiognomies that presented themselves as deceased, these dead men's words in resonant mouths, left him dazed—did not take his eyes off the most distressed of these knights, Brother Lahire.

The anteater continued to lick Ogier's hand and the young page offered no resistance: with absent gaze, he seemed frozen in a strange torpor.

"Withdraw your hand!" the Grand Master cried to him. But the youth no longer stirred.

Suddenly, the impatient Brother Lahire moves forward: he falls to his knees. Now enveloped by a luminous cloud the young boy offers himself to the eyes all in the perfect nudity of a virgin maid but, remarkably, retains an erect phallus. The Grand Master hurls himself backwards: the radiant creature receives the anteater's homage. A thundering voice declaims these word: *"In him I am pleased!"* All the knights prostrate themselves; a single cry is raised: *"Gloria in excelsis Baphometo!"* Then—but very far away—the cock crowed in the countryside; the glow faded at once, noisily.

Ogier stood up trembling in every limb: what did they want from him? Seeing them there all haggard, eyes rolling back inside their heads, arms reaching towards him, the young boy was truly terrified: fear twisted his stomach and he dreaded a loosening of the bowels, which would have earned him the Seneschal's whip; in fact it had been agreed with the latter that he should be back in his cell, neat and clean, before vespers.

Indeed, having been for centuries the object of a solicitation as assiduous as it was secret on the part of one or another of the dignitaries of the fortress at the time of the commemorative ceremony, he, knowing himself to be desirable—and this at an age when desire is still ambiguous, and when ambiguity, so natural at that age, at times confers on one a physiognomy as deceptive as his—was the first to revel in it for his own sake, from one celebration to the next, from eternity to eternity, even though, when leaving the *arms* of this or that Brother Breath, it meant passing into the breath of the Grand Master, who through him and unbeknownst to himself was dealing with "Theresa."

What could he possibly know about this saint? Lodged in the organ of that adolescent corpse which she thereby animated, the more her powers exhaled their celestial passion, the hotter the boy's ardor burned. It was her virgin powers that maintained Ogier's body between childhood and youth and kept it from passing into manhood. She herself was his life-flow, the enrichment of his prodigious semen, and she perpetuated the precocity of this self-sufficient puerile body. Thus Ogier took pleasure in his own charms, unaware that the modesty of a saint actually made his vices flourish and that the charity of a soul so precious drove him to surrender himself.

Entrusted with receiving the guests who ventured into this fortress—especially those whom the Grand Master assigned to his care, that he might ease their pains, pamper and soothe them until they became ex-haled upon his roseate mouth—in this manner he had also received the one who in the form of an anteater claimed he was called "Frederick." Some funambu-lists who exhibited the animal in public squares had brought it to the fortress; in all innocence Ogier had bought it from them and, having then lodged it in a stable and feeling no less concerned with finding it the proper food, he remembered having seen ants in some nearby underbrush and hastened to take his guest there. But there the anteater suddenly revealed himself to the young page as he really was: Ogier fainted.

Now in a dream he saw his own body floating near the vault of the walled-up oratory. And he experienced a most pleasant sensation from this, for hovering around him was a radiant beauty, unfolding long veils with which she concealed the naked corpse. Then the one hidden inside the anteater's form showed himself in his human state and, continuing to walk about on all fours, interrogated the radiant beauty:

"By the powers of Heaven, what are you doing in these musty parts?"

"O scorner of God, to what now have you been reduced! To you who misused such great gifts against Him, I, his servant, have only been a proud will, which I am but all too much in my own eyes as well! And now this same pride excludes me from the highest circles, and I remain attached to the souls that are dear to me! I lie in wait for their arrival at this fortress: once again I wish to save them from their wanderings, and in order to approach them I have no other choice but to assume the body of this child."

"How can that be?" asked the one whom the anteater's form concealed. "Both the means and the ends amaze me!"

"O lucid madman, you wish to usurp for yourself alone the kingdom of the Antichrist! Do you not know that love ennobles the ignoble places it inhabits!" she said, indicating the young boy.

Then the one they called Frederick the Antichrist said:

"He's a child of exquisite beauty: the nobility of his features consigned him to a tragic end. But in your raptures might you not have transgressed the dogma to the point of absorbing the separated soul of this adolescent as well? Indeed, where is it? Blessed or damned, will it never rejoin its own body again? Has it exchanged its own for yours? Will it resurrect in a saint's body? Or did he receive at birth the soul of a wicked old man who had to redeem himself in a second life and perish at the age of innocence before he could commit new crimes? Did this soul then pour its restlessness into the temperance of your own? And a few centuries later augment the malice of my own and relieve me of all the burden of teaching? What do the table-turnings of Jersey and Duino have to say about this?"

"O Frederigo! Here we know what it cost to form our visages, and if we do not change further we shall never be done paying the price of what we once were! I, who am less than nothing in this stillborn semen, I remain His servant such as He knows me—if He still wishes to recognize me! But was it not to spurn His grace that you denied even the image of the man He created walking erect? You can simulate an anteater as you please, but you shall remain Frederick for eternity!"

"Is that so! Might he also be the god responsible for the self of any anteater? But even then I could not escape him! Will I next don an ant's armor? And might there not be a god of ants that saves them from the anteater's hunger? Must one wait until he tells himself in turn: The anteater lives not by ants alone? . . . All the same, I'm better off in this anatomy than you could ever be in that puerile organ, O imperious woman!"

They argued thus with no end in sight until the bell pealed.

"Be advised," said the radiant beauty, "that your condition will be worse here than down below, for no one will understand you! They will interrogate you, for they also interrogate animals; they will torture you if you don't answer, for they also interpret the muteness of beasts; and they will make predictions from your cries and you will not even be able to defend

140

yourself! I shall lend you the voice of this child: it belongs to me and I myself move his tongue!"

"No, O generous soul! I do not wish to defend myself at all! For if I had to speak again, I should repeat shocking things which you would not dare to utter, were they even imputed to a mere anteater!"

"Go on, I shall faithfully translate your thoughts: charity knows not its own interests! But all that is condemned shall be made manifest, and all that is manifest is light!"

"But he whose light is darkness, what darkness!" began to sneer the man who obstinately walked on all fours. Then suddenly the anteater's form covered him completely again, and now only hissing these last words with its tensile, sticky tongue, it attacked the radiant figure and, too slowly for Ogier's liking, lifted her veils: for her voluptuous splendors had already begun to appear when Ogier suddenly saw again his own cadaver twitch at the end of a rope and open wide his staring eyes; he cried out so loudly that he awoke with a start.

He was not even surprised when he found himself on his cot in his cell, and none of the remarks exchanged in his dream remained in his memory. At that moment the bell pealed a second time, and Ogier, having washed and scented himself, ran with all haste to the banquet preparations where his duties commanded him. At the beginning of the meal he had been witness to Sir Jacques' consternation when the besiegers had issued their summons. But such movements of troops and investments of the fortress, which dissolved like snow once the ransom was delivered, were so common that Ogier had never paid much attention to them. So long as the matter involved only the incomprehensible demand for the extradition of

"Frederick the Antichrist," he thought it was merely one of the countless "codes" used by the Temple during conferences. But as soon as he understood—from rumors that were circulating from mouth to mouth—that this name was associated with a strange mammal allegedly hidden within the fortress, even before the Grand Master had summoed him the fear that the sudden discovery of his rare animal by the stable-boys might give a semblance of reason to the slander of the beseigers and cause some sort of riot among the numerous laborers in the enceinte on that day, if ever the knowledge of the unusual summons were to spread among that superstitious brood, prompted Ogier to go and fetch the beast straightaway, even before the Grand Master had summoned him. Without in the least suspecting who was really guiding his movements and inspiring his words,—in as much as the mysterious power inside him had not deprived him of his wits but was content only to drive him on—he told himself that the monster would amuse the noble guests and at the same time reassure the Grand Master: if they insisted on pursuing the joke of "extraditing" the alleged "Frederick," then Ogier would give him up for lost and, as the impromptu liberator of the Temple, would become the hero of this memorable day. Vain to the very tips of his fingernails, the beautiful child was anxious to give proof of another kind of power than that to which he was accustomed here. Later, the interrogation of "Frederick" by the Grand Master seemed part of some huge prank to him. Even so, finding it a bit long, he had dozed off, unaware that terrible spirits inhabited him and were making use of his voice.

Brother Damiens had seen nothing, if not that these knights were either giving themselves over to the last peripeties of a rite whose meaning escaped him, or simulating gestures in preparation for delirium, if they were not already engulfed in it. But, hiding behind a column, the more attentively to observe the page, he was asking himself if this young boy had so rehearsed his role as to be able to right himself slowly from his prone position without relinquishing his stiffness, or if an invisible force had set him thus back on his feet in such a manner that he remained inert, hands spread— when suddenly the boy, awakening and casting terrified glances around him, let his gaze come to rest on Brother Damiens. A batting of the lashes in his direction was enough to cause the Chaplain to think he too was losing his mind: a thick veil was rent inside him: whether Ogier would belong to him or he himself would belong to Ogier—no reasoning could resist the force that, through the boy's eyes, reclaimed him from the depths of time.

Through the page's eyes, in fact, Theresa thus contemplated that which she had long ago discerned in this soul whom a few words written by the saint's hand had consigned to the obstinate delectation of his own misfortune. Of this soul so many times shattered by aspirations, quarrels, compromises, jealousies, and anxieties shared with spirits to which by turns it had been joined over the centuries, there remained but the sterile vibration of an intention drained of motive. Either this vibration would reverberate his complaint from eternity to eternity, or Theresa, once again bringing the motive back to its original intensity, would thereby destroy the intention with a gesture still inconceivable to her own eyes, and, in separating her from him forever, would forever separate her from herself as well.

Thus inside the bosom of the young boy that she

animated, the saint underwent the ultimate test she had assigned herself, bound to the law that modifies the breaths among themselves, she herself being modified in Ogier, concealing the secret of the Holy Order: now absorbing the spirits of depravity into herself alone, she would clear a safe path for this pair of newly expired souls that she had vowed to unite at the moment of their dissolution; and liberating them from their own perversity, offering herself in blasphemy to their intention, she would free them of the blasphemy thereby consummated. If indeed she could confuse her own movements with those of the juvenile body she had usurped . . . he in the meanwhile might carry on the struggle that she made him fight against himself as long as she was there . . . .

Having no suspicion of how he had looked when he had just appeared, he was convinced, upon hearing them invoke him in unison by an incomprehensible name, that this cry was the designated signal that marked him as their prey: the last image of his nightmare came back to him: without a doubt, they were really going to hang him! At once he made ready to mount his animal, though it was quite slow; but as his eyes searched for it in vain among the knights frozen in prostration, he noticed a naked man in the mammal's stead, wearing the collar and walking on all fours. His vast forehead, turned towards the ground, overhung his fulminating eyes with tufted eyebrows while his lips disappeared beneath enormous mustaches that swept the flagstones: but no longer freely walking in circles, he came and went only as far as was permitted him by the stretched chain, the end of which was attached to a figure that had suddenly appeared on the threshold.

What followed culminated Ogier's confusion: for

advancing towards him, sparkling in a coat of mail, holding in one hand the naked man's chain and in the other a scale, was Valentine de Saint-Vit, hair flowing over her shoulders, breasts emerging out from under the silver mail, her visage stern, her lips and the nails of her supple fingers painted. Lifting the scale with one pan raised while the other hung down under an invisible weight, she said to the young page:

"O Theresa, behold the imbalance of the spheres you have caused by your voluntary exile! In the name of the Thrones and Dominions, resume your place in the space of spirits, return to complete the number of the elect and relinquish his body and visage to the soul of my nephew! I hereby liberate you from this sorcerer in the guise of a beast, whose rounds enclose you in the lower circles!"

But inside Brother Damiens someone, terrified, recognized the one who spoke thus: unaware of who was responsible for his having been formerly joined to her—for it was the voice of the woman whom the saint, in creating her as her own replica through her intercessions, had joined to him as companion during his last life—he nevertheless knew what he had done to this soul for her to dare to appear here with the attributes of celestial justice, which she seemed to wear with derision.

Now, however complicit each had been with the other in the world, when they expired the couple they had formed was disunited at once: scattered to these parts by the air currents, each of the two breaths sought some semblance of a supposite that might assume his own intention. Indeed every breath that expires, once it has become pure intention immediately forgets the motive; if a long-expired breath comes to invade it, the latter remembers what the oblivious breath had lived:

each one, deprived of its own motive, becomes the motive of the other's intention: one projects itself into the future, the other into the past. Astonishing indeed! Neither the one nor the other has any suspicion of their posthumous condition—Theresa allowed them this illusion. Thus from afar Brother Damiens suddenly saw himself as the witness of a future existence thereby elapsed in his own past. Drawn here by the anguish of his former victim, Valentine de Saint-Vit had invaded with her shadow the intention of her who was once the perverted companion of the one, now mute inside Brother Damiens, who was observing the scene from behind the column.

While she thus exhorts Theresa, at the same time her face and voice excite the body of the deceased youth. From the shudders of the organs of the young body she has occupied, the saint has guessed the ruse of the twofold demand: while in him the spirit of Theresa remains inflexible, the spasms and gasps of his last moments are revived inside Ogier; in his precociously extinguished senses the object of his tormented delight is rekindled: Valentine de Saint-Vit—so feigned this unexpected emissary of the Thrones and Dominions—was concealing her fallacious exhortation with her own destiny when stating the command: "Relinquish his body to the soul of my nephew!"

Ogier cannot not grasp the meaning of these inconceivable words: the more the saint in him rebels on hearing them, the more she pours her ire into the organs of the eternalized boy; and the more she agitates him, the greater is Valentine de Saint-Vit's power of seduction over him. Before this wondrous apparition, he recoils; words fail him; he closes his eyes; but, regaining possession of him in his agitation, the saint's spirit moves the boy's tongue.

146

"Was it your place, life of my life renounced, was it your place to recall me among the elect? You who so excel at deception, go feign my return, complete the number, and take my place among the spirits, enjoy their applause! Go on, do me this favor! What balance would you have me restore? Discard that scale! Unhappy woman! Wipe away the paint from your face and intimidate no more nor seek to corrupt the body of this young boy: it is enough that you have sacrificed him . . . . As long as I inhabit him, I shall take upon myself all of his impurities . . . ."

Here Valentine de Saint-Vit seemed unable to remain serious: bursting into insolent laughter she dropped her scale.

Yet as the boy was uttering these words with eyes closed, she who had assumed the attributes of heavenly justice, sensing that Theresa's spirit remained obstinately within the youth, modified her gestures and language: slipping her hand under his chin, she raised his face; at her touch Ogier shuddered, opened his eyes. Yet as Valentine de Saint-Vit rested her fine fingers on the boy's lips and cast him a stern glance:

"Ogier!" she cried. "What madness has seized you, that you no longer remember the Lady of Palençay, your aunt, tutor, and benefactress? Do you pretend to be possessed? How presumptuous! Without me, what would you have become? A brigand! But since you entered here, what indeed have you become? The disgrace of the house of Beauséant! Peddling your semen in order to conquer the Temple! . . ."

Hardly had she said this when out of the flagstones amidst the prostrated knights arose the torso of Malvoisie; with a single gesture of his outstretched arm he tore off several links of mail from between the thighs of

147

Valentine de Saint-Vit and exposed her shame: glowing red, the haughty dragon sprang forth.

At the sight of this, the young page staggers: for indeed, by her persistent presence in his puerile organs, the saint only rouses his dormant seeds all the more; at this moment she can neither stifle what his own ardor has revived nor uphold the boy's reason thereagainst, for she herself has blinded it. Still she inspires in him a semblance of wrath: beside himself, he reaches for his dagger and draws it, hurls himself forward at the monster that is threatening him enticingly. Yet the life-flow inside him has already overtaken his murderous gesture; his covetous desire has already exposed him when Malvoisie seizes him and, stripping him of his knife, before his eyes lops off the dragon's head.

So loudly did Valentine de Saint-Vit scream that the Brethren knights, awakened with a start, evaporated with her into the whirlwind of her cry. Once again Ogier savored with his ears this same prolonged cry beneath the vaults; once again, upon hearing it, his life-flow deceived itself; and believing himself to be alone with this cry echoing within himself, he abandoned himself; and thus he was already spreading forth into the empty space, when an unspeakable shame filled his breast: Sliding towards him from behind the pillar came Brother Damiens—who until that moment had not dared stir from there, for fear of disturbing those who here passed for uncertain shades

— — — —

"Was this the way we were to meet again?" I dared at last to ask him, while the young page, having delicately slipped a pair of pillows under my head and carefully tucked in the sheets of the vast, columned bed, and seeing that I feared he might withdraw, sat down at one end of the quilt, letting one leg dangle in the air while he sat on the other, knee bent, one foot under his buttock. Leaning his elbow against the bedstead, chin in the hollow of his right hand, a bracelet about his wrist, with the fingers of his free hand he toyed with the beads of a rosary extended along his thigh sheathed in black and white striped breeches.

The gaze in his velvety eyes was the same, as was the short, straight nose with its quivering wings, the full mouth with arched lips whose smile bared a glittering set of teeth, the dimpled cheeks—the whole mischievous expression which once so improperly accompanied the grave words she long ago pronounced to me. So true was this that it tormented me to see her solemnly raise that hand, which I would have liked to bite, knowing that she had better things to do than to reassert her unshakeable resolve to remain a nun.

Now he—chin steady in his girlish palm—was defying me with everything which in past times she would only let me glimpse in passing and then make disappear on the pretext of making a mutual holocaust to our eternities. Here in this chamber of meditation of the Temple he plunged me back into a state of vulnerability even more remote, yet suddenly immediate, as if he himself had been its cause, opening old scars whose itches and absurd wounds he knew well.

And thus attired in his becoming surcoat, which seemed to accentuate two unlikely breasts, slim-waisted and displaying the contours of his silky legs— like at the rise of the curtain on some infantile "historical" representation of a fin-de-siècle Thursday— he brought his fingers together with thieflike skill and suppleness in a peremptory gesture of denial:

"Brother Damiens—for such is the name you will bear during your stay at our fortress of the Temple— Brother Damiens, I am at your disposal this first night only to instruct you in everything you will need for your guidance among the Brethren knights. If you believe we have already met—but when could that have been?—I cannot hear of it, and I certainly am not permitted to speak to you of my person or even to tell you my name: such would be a grave offense! My duty is humbly limited to putting you on your guard against all thoughts that might distract you from the defense of your thesis, which the Brethren knights would be most grateful to hear; and with God's help I shall serve to drive away all cause for worry from your side, even any fear that might disturb your rest in this holy house."

He stopped, having got carried away with the emphatic manner in which he said what he had wanted to tell me, and then he lowered his voice:

"**Perhaps you are sad because** you were rather brusquely separated from your lovely wife, and because, when you were lodged at the women's hostelry, she didn't come to give you your evening kiss. Henceforth only through me will you be able to communicate with her. At your command, I shall fly to her with whatever message you wish!"

Jumping up from the end of the bed and approaching the head, he brought his charming face close to mine. Following upon his declaration of reserve, this assault of solicitude seemed suspect to me: did he want as well to concern himself with the greatest of my weaknesses, my dependence on Roberte? Once again I recalled some remote circumstance when, shortly after our marriage and not long before she left the world forever, she had come one evening to see Roberte and, as though congratulating herself then for having brought my senses to the point of fixation—a salutary state, according to her—she interjected at the moment of departure: "Roberte has wildly beautiful eyes!"

I gestured with my head that I had no messages to send to the women's hostelry. Then, before he had the time to realize what was happening, I grasped his wrist and squeezed it hard. He quickly freed himself and, returning to the foot of the bed, said:

"However inhuman may appear this measure of separating our guests from their wives when they bring them here—though it is the rule in all monastic communities—bear in mind that here, moreover, you are in a fortress of the Temple, in the home of soldier-monks, where any feminine presence—except in circumstances beyond our control: war, epidemics, or calamities that bring in great numbers of people in distress—is utterly undesirable and even more strictly forbidden than in the Trappist order! God forbid that the noble lady should suffer the insult of any suspicion whatsoever!—Nevertheless, until the approaching day when the Grand Master will celebrate the solemn anniversary of his martydom, during which he will lift the enclosure, your lovely wife will remain . . . sequestered!"

As I had not even the strength to express my astonishment, being still more astonished at the sway he held over me in announcing this news, he, remaining on the bed, moved up with his hands and knees on top of the quilt until he was at the level of my pillow:

"You are weary," he said. "You may sleep without fear of waking up too late for the conventual mass: I shall be your morning bell! I can even reveal to you in a dream the questions the examiners will put to you, though you yourself would then act out the dream before the jury . . . . For by now everyone here knows your thoughts, except for the meaning you decide to give them, which you yourself do not yet know."

Then, supporting himself with both hands against my right and left hands and dominating me with his mouth:

"I know you will not sleep until I have delivered the evening kiss to her on your behalf," he said, lightly unclenching his teeth. "See the sandglass there? When I return, it will be time for lights out!"

His lips stopped moving for several seconds, but an invincible force held me back. Then lying down at my side, first stroking his thigh then rolling the beads of

152

the rosary between his slender fingers, he began to speak again:

"The intentions you ascribe to me here, before you have even understood them to be directed towards you, do not concern you such as you have now become, newly arrived here this evening, lying in this bed, separated from your wife for the first time in a long time, divided among the different arguments to be put forward—but such as you once relinquished yourself by your own doing. The man you were then, we have taken him in among ourselves as our due, for from here—where we have been relegated to keeping a vigil (temporary as far as you are concerned, eternal as concerns events), even to the point of inhabiting any one of the dwellings assigned us by the Father—we shall henceforth oversee your better part in every one of you who are restless on the other side. But what is this better part? You know it as well as I, Brother Damiens; the Life showed it to Mary: by heeding the Life, Mary not only chose her better part, she is herself in the Life by virtue of this better part of herself. Martha for her own part desires to make herself better—bustling about, contributing, growing—but in so doing she loses sight of her better part: she thinks she is obliging the Life. She cannot tolerate the thought that the Life has always been there, asking nothing except that it be heeded. Of course Martha too had her better part, but for having wished to make it evident to her own eyes through her action, she deafened herself to the Life: for one is in the Life only without knowing so, and in it one need do nothing. Thus every man in his brief existence has known a moment of peace where, fulfilled by something perhaps utterly meaningless, he no longer desired anything nor concerned himself with tomorrow. But who has ever dared to live like the lily of the fields? Who has ever believed he surpassed Solomon in all his glory? Then he reaches the turning point where already he can no longer tolerate his peace, which has just begun. It was childish indeed, and too paltry! He's already ashamed of it! And he is afraid of living as a useless stranger among his supposed contemporaries. Is it his fault if he was born too soon or too late, at the time of the Antichrist rather than in the age of the idols, at a time when Christ Crucified and the idols of all nations and of all eras merely serve to enrich the merchants, after the abolition of serfdom rather than during the slave-trade, before or after the age of arena games, of mystery plays or of the silver screen, the age of barter or of holidays with pay, of palfreys or sleeping-cars, of zoos, zen or insecticide spray—in 1264 or 1964? Like it or not, he must accept the inevitable. He thinks himself renewed, he likes to be told he has matured, that he is more lucid, and at age sixty he feels lighter than at twenty or thirty and smiles at the old skins he has shed, believes himself rejuvenated as he contemplates the family he has built and, not content with having reproduced, he goes off to revel in those places where—the horror!—he once prostituted his wife . . . . He forges ahead with his century!"—he continued, sighing deeply and running his lovely fingers over his long eyelashes as if to wipe away a tear, while the black and white plumes of his cap trembled with his indignation.

"And yet," he resumed, "when he was still but a useless stranger, he did not know that for us he was anything but this, that these places were open to him, the myriad intelligences returned here since the beginning of time . . . . What am I saying, he still would not know he was moving farther and farther

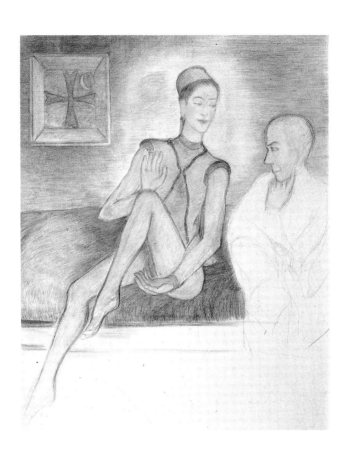

3. *Le jeune page provoquant Frère Damiens.*

"Feel me now and see whether or not I possess these cheeks, these hands, these thighs which look so appetizing to you, so pleasant to look at under this costume, though they are nothing but air. . . ." (Page 157) away from our dwellings, condemned to disowning himself every time his better part weighed him down, to fleeing himself from one day to the next, to believing himself still alive even after his very bones had begun to rot, if we hadn't taken that better part which for an instant he was himself, and had not grafted it like a cutting onto the Tree of Life."

Whether or not he had memorized this sort of sermon he was reciting, or whether on the contrary he was improvising it and, watching me out of the corner of his eye, managed to slip in several pious impertinences mixed with allusions to some obscure doctrine, everything—even the manner in which he sidled up to me only to turn away at my touch, at my slightest movement under the sheets—seemed to urge me not to spare an innocence so manifestly lacking in him, so strongly did I sense a tacit offer on his part.

He jumped down from the bed and, hands on his hips, slowly withdrew towards the back of the high chamber; showing only the balanced profile of his face, his beautiful eyes gazing up towards the vault, his lips half-open as if awaiting a reply, he raised his arms then let them fall back down with a kind of self-conceit as his bracelets and the beads of his rosary jingled audibly. Then halting his step, he showed only the back of his slender form, the shapely buttocks in their breeches. For a moment I would have esteemed him as much for this pose as for his words, but then he set down his cap and faded entirely into the shadow, where I then could make him out on his knees, saying his rosary. But almost at once his contours reappeared in the flickering light of the torches and, smiling with his white teeth, eyes flashing, and seeming amused by his decision to come back, he made a gesture of appeasement with his palms:

"Of course, you have pursued a laudable intent: to discharge a sort of debt to the Order of the Temple for the promise, made very long ago, to achieve rank among the Brethren knights, the failure to do which would in no wise have been held against you! Now that you are here, as our guest, in this bed," and, folding his arms, he thrust one knee across the quilt towards my body, all the while remaining on his feet, "may I make so bold as to remind you that no one remembers a debt so well as he who would raise a new loan? All the same, you are free to defend your thesis or not: it is not indispensable to the rank to which you aspire, especially as it's all just a form of amusement to the rest of us. Whether or not you have demonstrated the state of indifference in which souls separated from their bodies exist as they await resurrection—might it be because this sort of question matters so little to the people of your century that you have come here to debate it in this old fortress of the Temple where an eternity has passed since the rusted swords cut short the final ends?—I fear that just as you had no luck convincing bodies temporarily united with their souls, you will have no more with the souls separated from them—also temporarily, you will tell them, temporarily!" and, staring at me, his eyes in mine, with a gaze so unbearable that I buried my head in the pillow: "—Believe me, the lack of interest here is at the very least as total as it is down there. When one leaves one's body, that's the last of one's worries! As for me, I left mine centuries ago, before I'd even turned fourteen: do you think I could ever have spoken to you in this fashion if I wasn't some little supernumerary in a play? For one of two things must be true: Either you have come here as one comes to a theatre—in which case, what is the use of discussing so serious a subject in such a place? Or else you wanted to make yourself heard by the separated souls; but then, what could a problem they have already resolved possibly mean to them? Appearing, disappearing, reappearing: do I need a body for such things? All those things are quickly done which within the body could only be accomplished with great difficulty. Here one enjoys before even wanting; one possesses, before the wish!" he said, while his palms, upturned in an unequivocal gesture, seemed all the more voluptuous, and his eyes sparkled.

"Just now when you seized my wrist, I had to escape your grasp because you hadn't heard me out entirely. If you thought you felt anything even remotely palpable—I am obliged to tell you—then your presence here is out of place: you are abusing the Grand Master's hospitality!" Then, more brusquely: "You have only one thing in mind, that your wife should come here and join us—is that not so?—and that the three of us should go to bed together. Your thesis defense is only a way for you to prove that I'm a whore. O Brother Damiens, it is hard to hear such words! All the same, playing dead among the living still passes; but playing the living among the dead, come now!"

Then, as if he had not yet done with adding to his charm by knitting his brows in anger, he immediately grew calm, still blushing however:

"Feel me now and see whether or not I possess these cheeks, these hands, these thighs which look so appetizing to you, so pleasant to look at under this costume, though they are nothing but air . . . ."

"No, I will not touch you!" I said, at the peak of my

desire. "For, if at the risk of lying I assert that I feel you to be fully fleshed, you will declare me unworthy of being received; if on the contrary I lie, at the risk of being cast into the shadows outside, my conscience will betray me! But if for some reason unknown to me you are impalpable after all, and I recognize this to be so, I have no guarantee that you will not be free to claim that I am lying for fear of being excluded, for it is very possible that, despite my lack of perception, you exist nevertheless . . . . It is easiest just to believe you."

"You don't believe it at all, venerable Brother! Now you are indeed lying! Why ascribe to me so devious a spirit as your own? And how to anticipate at any cost what would happen then? If you had said from the start that I am flesh and blood, I would have obeyed you there and then!"

"Ah!" I said, "if you are neither a spirit nor a whore, between the two there is plenty of room for a rogue!"

"Alas, Brother Damiens, you should have treated me like one! I've been waiting an eternity for that to happen, but for an eternity I have only been told so!"

With these words, I broke through my reserve; and I was about to reach out and seize him—when an irresistible torpor overcame me.

He had placed his hand on my forehead, and with his thumb and forefingers he lowered my eyelids while I inhaled a sweet odor of moisture from the hollow of his silky palm. Unable to reopen my eyes, I nevertheless saw him all the more distinctly before me: the bracelet on his delicate wrist, the velvet of his sleeve and, through the spaces between his tapered fingers resting on my eyelids, the oval of his visage and the luxuriant head of hair covered by his cap with black and white plumes.

He paused a moment, hand on my forehead, closing his eyes in turn, but then a smile carved the dimples back into his peach-colored cheeks.

As I was no longer stirring, he left the bed, extinguished the torches and lighted a night-lamp. Tossing aside his cap, he drew his dagger and stuck it into the wood of the low door. Then, removing the rosary from his belt, he wound it around his neck and wrists, and with his outspread hands he stretched it taut to the right and left until it formed a triangle. He seemed to strain his outstretched arms, then fell stiffly onto the flagstones.

No sooner was he lying thus on his back than he was slowly raised above the floor and up to the vault; floating in this horizontal position, he gently lowered himself onto the bed, where, crosswise, neck and wrists still bound by his rosary, he remained motionless.

Notes and Explanations
for *The Baphomet*

4. *La supreme vision de Frère Damiens.*

". . . he gently lowered himself onto the bed, where, crosswise, neck and wrists still bound by his rosary, he remained motionless." (Page 159)

I had just completed the last part of *Lois de l'hospitalité* when, during our summer sojourn in 1964 at the chateau of Chassy, I felt a desire to recapture certain emotions of my adolescent years. The result was the episode of young Ogier offering himself to Damiens, initially published under the title of "La Chambre de Meditation" in *Le Nouveau Commerce* (Autumn-Winter 1964). This text, which was destined later to serve as the Epilogue to *The Baphomet*, prompted me to write the Prologue (which appeared in the review *Mercure de France* in December of the same year). The whole thing was composed very quickly, as though all I had to do was transcribe a dictation, or better yet, *as though I were describing it as a play I was watching*, leaving out none of the

Excerpts from a letter by the author to Jean Decottignies published in an afterword to the latter's important monograph *Klossowski*, Editions Henry Veyrier, Jean-François Bory ed.

163

words which the actors' *various poses* suggested to me, so that I actually felt as though I were *right there* listening to them speak.

The idea of writing an historical novel evoking the circumstances of the destruction of the Order of the Temple by Philip the Fair revived the very distant memories of my reading of Walter Scott at age thirteen, in Geneva. Perhaps it is unnecessary to point out that the names of two of the characters of the Prologue, Bois-Guilbert and Malvoisie, are borrowed from two Templars in *Ivanhoe*. So much for the appearance of the historical genre. As for the roots of the essentially theological questions: What happens to souls once they are separated from their bodies? Do they or don't they lose their identities? Do they know the state of indifference—indeed, of total *oblivion*—or do their earthly intentions continue to exist only in the state of *intensity* and, bereft of their bodies, do they no longer experience any obstacles to their mutual interpenetration, until the day of Judgment which will reunite them with their own bodies? These are the questions that inspire the discussions and dealings of my characters, and as a result in a general way *The Baphomet* reflects to a large extent my affinities with the great heresiarchs of Gnosticism (Valentinus, Basilides, Carpocrates) and shows, on the level of form and *mise en scène,* the influence of the *Oriental tale* (Blanchot *dixit*) of Beckford's *Vathek* . . . .

Distinguishing between the Baphomet
and the Antichrist

The *Baphomet* has diverse etymologies. I have not retained the one put forward by Albert Olivier, whereby the term derives from a mispronunciation of the name of Mahomet. On the other hand, the three phonemes that constitute the denomination are also said to signify, in coded fashion, *Basileus philosophorum metaloricum*: the sovereign of metallurgical philosophers, that is, of the alchemical laboratories that were supposedly established in various chapters of the Temple. The androgynous nature of this figure apparently goes back to the Adam Kadmon of the Chaldeans, which one finds in the Zohar. Instead of the bearded androgyne of Saint-Merri, my story preferred to expand upon the statements of a lay brother at the time of the trial, which explained one of the pieces of evidence, a golden head containing the skull of a virgin, as justifying the accusation of idolatry. Hence my invention of the boy Ogier, who is fated to simulate this supposed idol.

There is no proof that the Templars were ever charged with professing the heresy of the Docetes, who claimed that Christ was not born, did not die or resurrect except in appearance. In the state of being *breaths* in which my characters find themselves, it is their *forgetfulness of ever having had a body* which leads them to this heresy—of which fact only the Grand Master, Theresa d'Avila, Damiens, and above all the revived Ogier are aware.

The Antichrist is an apocalyptic premonition of the Epistles of St. John of Patmos, inspired by a statement by Christ (Matthew XXIV): "For there shall arise false Christs and false prophets, and shall shew great signs and wonders; insomuch that, if it were possible, they shall deceive the very elect." It is as well a role ascribed to various historical figures such as Frederick II von Hohenstaufen, King of Sicily and hostile to the Crusades, who favored Jews and Arabs in his court; Popes and Antipopes also denounced one another by the same term before Luther qualified the Pope in Rome in the same fashion, and finally Nietzsche resolutely laid claim to the role of Antichrist for himself. Hence the mistake made by the Grand Master when he believes he is dealing with Frederick, King of Sicily, who had said upon seeing a wheatfield, "How many gods grow here!" (a mocking reference to the consecration of the host); the anteater replies: "I said more than that," etc.

There should be no confusion between the figure of the Baphomet and that of the Antichrist. To liken the two is to lose the entire thread of my plot.

By means of the timeless space of the *breaths,* the characters of Sir Jacques de Molay, Theresa d'Avila and finally Nietzsche and Damiens are juxtaposed around the page Ogier as so many historically different worlds occurring simultaneously.

The Grand Master represents the Gothic sensibility, contrary to St. Theresa, who arises from the Baroque world, while the young Ogier, in the rotation of his imputrescible body, signifies as it were the transition from ogival thought to the spiraling Baroque sensibility, which reintroduces sensuality into the contemplative experience of the Spanish mystics (evocation of Bernini's statue of St. Theresa).

The difference between the Gnostic notion of expiatory reincarnation and the Nietzschean Eternal Return

The Baphomet (gnosis or fable, or Oriental tale) should in no way be seen as a demonstration of the substratum of truth in the semblance of doctrine that is Nietzsche's Eternal Return, nor as a fiction constructed on this personal experience of Nietzsche.

On the other hand, my book purports to take into

consideration the theological consequences thereof (i.e., a soul's travels through different identities), as these coincide with the metempsychosis of Carpocrates's gnosticism—to which the character of Theresa d'Avila gives some manner of credence in her prayers when she beseeches God to grant the respite of a new existence, that is, of subsequent reincarnations, to the soul of Damiens.

In the context of my book, this paradoxical episode does not invalidate, but actually confirms divine prescience in Theresa's spirit: her soul, despite the various individualities it will pretend to assume, will remain the same, unchanged, in its essence. Such is the contradiction inherent to the fable of the Baphomet: the breaths simulate metamorphoses, always unwittingly, by virtue of the supposed "pact of the Prince of Modifications with the Creator," while the main protagonists, the Grand Master, Theresa d'Avila, the young Ogier, Frederick the Antichrist and Damiens, always remain themselves.

The Masonic style of commemoration

The series of phantasmagorical sequences in the book (chapters V, VI, VII) is interpolated between chapters IV and VIII and their description of the events of the commemoration, which in chapter VIII extends in three sections up to the epilogue.

To what corresponds this interpolation (of alternations of memory and oblivion) between the peripeties of the solemn ceremony which necessarily supposes the return of their memories to all the participants, who are moreover temporarily endowed with their bodily appearance? Essentially, it corresponds to the

Masonic style (already discernible in the remarks exchanged with the supposed Baphomet and yet again in those made among the guests of the Grand Master): the replies to trick questions; the dialogue between Sir Jacques and Philip the Fair; the sham beheading of the King (a reminiscence of the ritual execution of the murderer of Hiram, builder of Solomon's Temple). In my book this is, if you will, a spectacular parody that nevertheless preserves all the symbolic gravity of the purposely absurd actions and words, and is thus a test of the intuition of truth and falsity for the Brethren, who aspire to higher degrees of initiation.

Ogier revived

No different from the way he was in the action of the Prologue, young Ogier reappears as Lahire's and Malvoisie's page at the commemoration, serving the table of the Grand Master. Initiated long before by Malvoisie to the rites of his enthronement in the Prologue, he is conscious only of himself, his charm, and the seductiveness he has over the community of Brethren knights, *and has no conception whatsoever of his own transformation into the Baphomet*, except that he remains haunted by the idea of being hanged anew. ("It was to be adored . . . that I had myself hanged. And hanged, I found myself adorable, adoring myself as I awaited an adorer.")

The Epilogue

Have I not said that in writing out the action of this book I felt I was watching a play?

The curtain rises again, this time on a room of the hostelry of the Temple, which survives to this day like any other monastery of a contemplative nature. In this rather vast room illuminated by torchlight, a guest lies abed. At the end of the bed sits a young man, dressed in a silken medieval page's costume and playing with a rosary between his fingers.

Between the character of the young Ogier of the plot and the young costumed boy who seems identical to Ogier as for his age, bearing and charm, there is supposed to be a considerable difference, to judge by the narrator's perplexity when the page claims to know him as Brother Damiens. Already in the final scene Brother Damiens, while witnessing the incomprehensible hallucination of the Brethren knights, wonders whether Ogier had rehearsed his role in those circumstances.

Here the narrator, listening to the boy speak—initially the only one to speak—seems to ask himself the same question: has someone dictated to him the sermon he is reciting, which he seems to have learned by heart? Might they not have had him rehearse, before acting out for his guest, his ever more provocative gestures? The boy, moreover, seems to guess this and suggest it all the more by his denials. *"Appearing, disappearing, reappearing: do I need a body for such things?"* Hence the lively exchange of remarks and the young page's rejoinder, which is as incongruous as it is cruel: *"If you had said from the start that I am of flesh and blood, I would have obeyed you there and then!"*

Did Brother Damiens really come to defend his thesis in a "theatre"? Might this be another instance of the parody implicit in masonic initiations? Or, not knowing the code, might he have interpreted wrongly,

that is literally, the young page's admonition: *"Do
you think I could ever have spoken to you in this
fashion if I wasn't some little supernumerary in a
play?"*

Table of Illustrations

Plate No. 1:

Malvoisie initiant le leune Ogier aux secrets du temple, 1987. Colored pencil on paper. 137 X150 cm. Courtesy Galerie Lelong, Zürich.

Plate No. 2:

L'esprit du Grand Maître explorant le corps imputrescible de jeune Ogier, 1982. Colored pencil on paper. 252 X 150 cm. Courtesy Galerie Lelong, Paris.

Plate No. 3:

Le jeune page provoquant Frère Damiens, 1986. Colored Pencil on paper. 136 X 86 cm. Courtesy Galerie Beaubourg, Paris.

Plate No. 4:

La supreme vision de Frère Damiens, 1987. Colored pencil on paper. 148 X 86 cm. Courtesy Galerie Lelong, Zürich.

173

The Eridanos Library

Eridanos Press, Inc., P.O. Box 211, Hygiene, CO 80533.

This book was printed in July of 1988 by
Il Poligrafico Piemontese P.PM. in Casale Monferrato, Italy.
The Type is Baskerville 12/14.
The paper is Corolla Book 120 grs. for the insides
and Acquerello Bianco 160 grs. for the jacket,
both manufactured by Cartiera Fedrigoni, Verona,
especially for this collection.